Jamie and the Mystery Quilt

Look for these and other Apple Paperbacks in your local bookstore!

Jamie and the Mystery Quilt

Vicki Berger Erwin

AN
APPLE
PAPERBACK

SCHOLASTIC INC.
New York Toronto London Auckland Sydney

ISBN 0-590-44009-8

13 12 11 10 9 8 7 6 5 4   2 3 4 5/9

Printed in the U.S.A.   28

First Scholastic printing, April 1987

To Jim.

1

Jamie huddled, shivering, in the corner of the porch swing, and picked small flakes of paint off the railing. She had only a few minutes to call her own before her sister returned home from school.

Two boys ran toward the house, then paused at the foot of the walk. The biggest poked his friend and whispered loud enough for Jamie to hear, "Go ahead, I dare you to ring the doorbell."

Jamie sat motionless, hidden in the shadow of a large oak, waiting to see what they had in mind.

The smaller boy hung back, staring at the shabby, rambling house, eyes wide and fists clenched tightly at his sides.

"Chicken!" his companion taunted.

"I don't think it's really haunted," Jamie heard the little one say, his voice quivering.

"Huh! Look at that spooky tower up there . . . and those shutters all falling down . . . and look at all the paint coming off. Nobody but a ghost or a witch would live in a crummy house like that!"

Jamie's heart pounded. How dare they insult her house! Ghost in the tower! Ridiculous! That was her special place. She'd show those boys.

She dropped her foot to the porch and pushed off, making the swing's unoiled hinges creak eerily. The boys looked at one another and without a word scurried down the street.

Jamie pressed her fist tight against her mouth. Her straight brown hair fell around her face like a veil. Did little kids really think their house was haunted? It needed work, she was the first to admit it, but. . . .

She heard feet scraping along the sidewalk. They were coming back. Her brown eyes blazed with anger. She'd tell those little brats a thing or two if they dared bad-mouth her house again. Jamie stood up and pushed the swing against the wall of the house.

"Hi, Jamie!" her little sister, Cindy, yelled, waving wildly.

Her anger evaporated. She waved back. She had no time to waste now. It was up to her to keep things going until Mom returned home from work.

"Hey, guess what?" Cindy said.

"Hey yourself." Jamie ran down the steps to greet her sister. "What? Tell me what right now. I don't think I can wait another minute! Tell me!

Tell me!" she teased, putting her arm around Cindy, and leading her into the house.

"Oh, you!" Cindy pushed Jamie away as soon as they got inside. She tugged off her coat and gloves and piled them on the bench in the entry hall. Jamie hung hers in the closet, and motioned for her sister to do the same.

Cindy shivered. "Brrr, it's almost as cold in here as it is out there." She wrapped her arms around her body and rubbed.

"I'll turn up the heat in a minute. Remember, we decided there was no sense in keeping the house heated when we were gone. But go on up and get our sweaters anyway. It doesn't get that warm even with the furnace going."

Cindy ran up the stairs. Jamie headed for the kitchen, stopping to turn up the thermostat. Hot cocoa might help warm them while they waited for the house to heat up. She also needed to check on what Mom had planned for supper.

Jamie poured milk into a pan and set it on the stove. Cindy came in with the sweaters just as the milk began to bubble around the edges.

"Are you ready to listen to my news now?" Cindy asked.

"Yes, I really am now. Tell me all about it."

"I get to be a fairy in the school play," Cindy announced, her eyes glowing.

"That's great!" Jamie said.

Cindy was an obvious choice to play a fairy, with her golden curls, blue eyes, and rosy cheeks marked by deep dimples on either side of her mouth. Jamie loved her beautiful little sister, but she sometimes felt it was a little unfair that Cindy had gotten every one of their mother's good features, while she had inherited all her looks from their dad — tall and angular with brown hair, brown eyes, and not a hint of a dimple anywhere.

"I get to wear a costume, too," Cindy continued. "It's going to be blue with silver sparkles and a crown and lace." She stared into her cocoa.

"Oh?" Jamie felt a tiny seed of apprehension sprout inside her. "Where do you get this wonderful costume? At school?"

"No, not exactly," Cindy said reluctantly, spinning her spoon around in her cup. "We have to get our own costumes."

Jamie sighed. Even Cindy knew how tight money was right now.

"Do you think I can, Jamie?" the little girl asked hopefully. "It can't cost very much, can it?"

"We'll talk to Mom tonight. Don't worry about it," she said, seeing her sister's face fall. "And I think they made a perfect choice." She gave Cindy a quick hug.

"Right now I think you'd better check this out." Jamie nodded toward the bulletin board where

Mom posted jobs for them every day.

"Okay, okay," Cindy groaned. "You know, we practiced all day and I'm a little tired."

"Cindy. . . ."

Before Jamie could begin to lecture, Cindy darted away and made herself look very busy.

Jamie opened the refrigerator to take out the ingredients to start dinner. She let her thoughts go back to their problems with the house. What needed to be done to get it fixed up? The white paint had peeled away until the house looked gray, and some of the shutters needed to be nailed back up. The yard needed so much work that even now, in the middle of winter, it was overgrown with weeds.

But, Jamie thought, the house still had a certain look about it — a look that newer houses couldn't begin to come close to. The porch was wide; the trim beautifully carved. Fan-shaped windows sparkled over the front door and marked the staircase landing.

And above it all was the tower. A short flight of stairs led from the library Dad had used for an office to a square tower that was filled with light no matter what time of day it was. She sometimes felt as if she could see everywhere when she was up that high. Jamie didn't think she could survive without her tower. Even though it was hot in summer and cold in winter, it was her favorite place in the whole world and she would do anything to keep it.

"Girls! Anyone home?" Mom called out cheerily from the front hall.

Jamie grabbed a towel and went to the kitchen doorway. "Hi, Mom. Glad you're here." When Mom joined her, Jamie leaned over to give her a hug.

"Where's Cindy?" Mom asked, looking around.

"Probably upstairs practicing to be a fairy. She got a part in the school play. Ooops." Jamie clapped her hand over her mouth. "I should have let her tell you."

"Don't worry," Mom said. "I'll act surprised."

Cindy rushed into the room just then and threw herself at Mom. "Guess what?" she said breathlessly. Without waiting for an answer she continued, "I get to be a fairy in the play at school! I get a blue costume and a crown. I even have my very own poem to say."

"That's wonderful, darling! I'm so proud of you. You'll be a perfect fairy." Mom patted Cindy on the back.

"But," Cindy pulled away so she could see her mother's face, "we have to make our own costumes."

Mom ran her fingers through her short, blond hair, then shook it out, making the curls dance madly. Without answering, she walked into the kitchen. Cindy and Jamie followed behind.

"I'll talk to your teacher, Mrs. Crockett, about it," she finally said.

"Thanks, Mom." Cindy looked at her mother, eyes full of trust, then skipped off.

Jamie joined her mom. "Dinner's almost ready. How was your day?"

"About the same. We got in some new mysteries you might be interested in. I'll bring them home as soon as they're processed."

Mom was a librarian in the city library. Jamie, an avid reader, loved the little extras her mom's job allowed them — like getting first pick of all the new books.

"I also received a call from the realtor, Mr. Payne, who did the appraisal on the house. What he said we could sell this place for!" Mom said, stroking the carved door frame.

"Sell the house?" Jamie stared at her mom, her mouth hanging open. "I thought you just wanted to know what it was worth for taxes or something. You never said anything about selling."

"I haven't done anything yet, Jamie. After all, this was your dad's home. Someone from his family has always lived here. I hate to be the one to let strangers move in."

"Well, I've been doing some thinking, too," Jamie replied. "Since we could use some extra money, how would you feel about my getting a job after

7

school? I know I wouldn't make much, but. . . ."

"Honey, you know I need you to take care of Cindy."

"I wouldn't do anything that would interfere with that. I've already put my name on a list to do tutoring. I could do that here. Or I could baby-sit."

"That's a nice offer, but you don't understand. It just takes so much to keep a house like this up. Ever since Dad died, it's gotten worse. Now we not only have to buy the materials, but we have to hire someone to do the work."

Not giving Jamie a chance to say anything, Mom continued, "And do you know how much the cost of gas has gone up? We've shut off every room we don't use, and we still are paying *twice* as much for heat as we used to pay when we had all the rooms open and warm. I don't know how much longer we can do it.

"Cindy wants a costume. A costume for a play and I don't know if we can afford it. But if we got rid of this place, we wouldn't have to worry about things like that."

Jamie's hands were shaking so much she almost dropped the salad bowl she was carrying to the sink. She put it down and wiped her hands on a dish towel. Her mom couldn't possibly mean what she was saying.

"I think it's a bit much to sell the house so Cindy

can be in a play, Mom. Surely we can find something around here to use to make her costume," she added quickly.

"I wasn't suggesting we sell the house to pay for Cindy's costume. I was just pointing out how bad things are."

"I couldn't live anyplace else," Jamie said. "I love the house so much! I'd give up anything, *anything* to keep it."

"College?" Mom asked.

"That's a long way off. Who knows what may happen before then? And what about that woman who called the other day from the Historical Society?" Jamie persisted. "The one who wants to include our house in the historical tour — Mom, it's a *landmark*."

"Jamie, this house is a wreck. We'd never get it ready in time. What it needs is an owner who has plenty of money and know-how to take care of an old home like this."

The entire conversation was beginning to ruin Jamie's appetite. She had to change the subject.

"You might find a rich husband," Jamie said, teasing.

Mom pushed her glasses down her nose and looked over the top of them at Jamie. "Just what we need, another mouth to feed."

They both laughed.

"You know what though?" Mom went on. "I

think I can find something around here to make Cindy's costume. There are boxes and boxes of old clothes and things in the attic. I even have a crown she can wear."

"A crown?" Jamie wondered what she could possibly be talking about.

"Mom, is dinner ready?" Cindy asked, joining them. "Are you talking about my costume?"

"Yes, I'm telling Jamie about the crown I'm going to let you wear." Mom turned her attention back to the stove.

Cindy stared at her mother. "Does it have diamonds?" she asked.

Her mother smiled. "They look like diamonds. No one will ever know the difference. We're going to find some old dresses that we can cut up for your costume, and you'll be all set."

"It has to be blue," Cindy reminded her.

"We'll find something blue," Mom said.

Jamie set the bowl of lettuce she had been tearing on the table, then checked the casserole in the oven. It was bubbling, so she took it out. "Dinner's ready," she announced.

Before she could even sit down, the telephone rang.

"I'll get it," Jamie said, rushing to the phone. "Hello?"

"May I speak to Jamie Huddleston, please?" a masculine voice asked.

"This is Jamie."

Her palms began to sweat.

"This is Kevin Parker."

Jamie's stomach turned over twice as it traveled to her toes and back up again.

"I was talking to Miss Ryan today and she suggested you might be available to help me out with my math. I'm having some problems." Kevin sounded embarrassed.

Jamie's stomach stabilized as a combination of disappointment and relief flooded over her. What else would someone as popular as Kevin possibly want from her but help with his homework?

"I'm willing to pay to have you tutor me," he added, filling in the pause.

"Oh, yeah, sure. I'd be glad to help. I told Miss Ryan I'd like to do some tutoring."

"I need to get started soon, so I can make up some tests before the quarter ends. Would tomorrow be all right?" Kevin asked.

"That would be fine if you don't mind coming to my house. I have to watch my little sister until my mom gets off work," Jamie replied. "You can come right after school and we can get in a good hour or so of work."

"Sounds good."

"First we'll get an idea of where you need help," Jamie said, voicing the plans she was already starting to make.

"Just about everywhere, I'm afraid," Kevin admitted. "I'll see you tomorrow then."

"Wait," Jamie practically yelled into the phone. "Do you know where I live?"

"I'll find it," he assured her before hanging up.

Jamie hurried back to the table.

"I have my first tutoring job," she announced excitedly.

"Jamie, I said you didn't have to do that." Her mother sighed.

"But I want to," Jamie insisted. "It won't pay the heating bill or anything like that, but it will come in handy for something. And anyway, my first 'client' is Kevin Parker."

"Who's he?" Cindy asked.

"He's an eighth grader! And he's cute enough and popular enough — I would almost be willing to pay to help him," Jamie said frankly, then wished she could bite her tongue off. Whatever possessed her to say something like that in front of blabbermouth Cindy? "Don't you dare say anything to him about what I just said," she warned her sister.

Cindy shrugged.

Jamie looked quickly at her mother to see what she was thinking. "Mom, will you please tell Cindy to leave us alone?"

She turned to Cindy. "If you don't, Mom and I won't help you with your costume."

"Cindy, you behave when Kevin is here. He and

Jamie will be doing homework, so don't bother them."

The look Mom gave Cindy said twice as much as her words, but it didn't stop Cindy from adding, "I'll bet they do homework. Kevin's an eighth grader! He's *experienced*."

"What do you know about experience?" Jamie said.

"If he's in the eighth grade, how come you're tutoring him?" Mom asked.

"I'm in advanced math. He must be in regular."

"Maybe it will be good for you," Mom said.

"What?" Jamie asked, puzzled.

"Having something to do besides homework and worrying about this house."

"Oh Mom, he's just coming to study. I'm not the type of girl he hangs around with."

"I want you to do my costume tonight," Cindy whined.

"I'm too tired," Mom said. "We'll have to do it on Saturday. No telling how many boxes we'll have to paw through before we find something."

"It'll be fun," Jamie said. "I love looking at all the stuff up there."

"Good, I appoint you chief looker," her mom said, rising to stack the dirty dishes.

"I'm going to help," Cindy chimed in.

"We'll need you," Mom said. "Just as we need you right now to help with the dishes."

13

Cindy made a face.

"Mom, I don't have much homework tonight. I'll start going through stuff now, if you don't mind," Jamie offered.

Cindy grabbed her mom around the legs. "Oh, please, Mom, please, please."

Mom looked reluctant.

"I want to, really," Jamie added.

"I guess it will be okay, but wear a sweater — it's like a freezer in the attic," she yelled after Jamie, who was already on her way up the stairs. "And be sure to leave enough time for a shower. It's filthy up there!"

2

Jamie turned the doorknob of the door leading to the third-floor attic. It wouldn't budge. She yanked on it and still it stuck tight. "Mom!" she yelled over the railing, "I think the door's locked or something!"

"In my jewelry case!" Mom answered.

"What?"

"The key is in my jewelry box." Mom appeared, making yelling no longer necessary.

Jamie darted into her mother's room and soon came out with the key to unlock the door.

Cindy crowded in so close, Jamie almost had to knock her out of the way to get the key in the lock. As soon as the door opened, she and Cindy pushed and shoved one another, trying to be the first one up the stairs. Their footsteps echoed against the wooden steps, drowning out their laughter.

When they arrived at the top of the staircase, Cindy stopped, her face mirroring her awe at the

15

collection of boxes, trunks, and furniture scattered everywhere.

"It's been a long time since I've been up here," Mom said from behind Jamie, startling her.

"There's too much stuff!" Cindy wailed.

Jamie faced her mom. "I thought you were tired."

"I was until I thought of all the goodies we might find, not to mention the mess you might leave if no one is here to remind you to straighten up."

"You're worried about *us* making a mess up here?" Jamie laughed. She pushed cobwebs out of her way, then bent over to examine some of the furniture that blocked their way.

"You know, this is kind of pretty," she said, wiping dust off the legs of a chair so she could examine the carvings.

Mom shrugged. "I guess. It's what some people would call antique." She pushed a table and another chair out of the way to make a path.

Jamie followed, checking each piece her mom set aside. "With this moved down, we *could* make the downstairs look just like the pictures of historical houses," she mumbled.

"Mom, Jamie isn't helping. She's not going to find anything looking at that old stuff," Cindy complained.

"What are you doing that's so much help?" Jamie countered, looking at her sister perched on the edge of a trunk looking over Mom's shoulder.

"Girls!"

"Okay, I'll look for something to use to make the costume first." Jamie turned away from the furniture and opened the first box she came to. She promised herself that she would come back and look at the furniture the first chance she had. She had a spark of an idea about what they might be able to do with this "junk."

"Look through all the boxes and trunks and pull out anything blue," Mom directed. "After we finish going through it all, we'll see if anything's worthwhile."

Inside the first box Jamie opened were three stacks of carefully folded men's clothing: one pile of shirts, one of pants, and one of jackets. She picked up a jacket and shook it out. Dust flew everywhere.

"Oh, brother!" Jamie dropped the jacket and waved her hand in front of her. Along with the dust came a strong odor.

"That's camphor. I imagine it was some kind of moth repellent," Mom said. "There are all kinds of moth balls in this box."

"Why are we keeping all this stuff?" Jamie asked, quickly looking through each stack. Finding only men's clothes, she closed it and moved on.

"I don't know. It's just always been here. Your dad's family seems to have made it a habit to keep everything."

"Look at this." Mom held up a maroon, polished-cotton dress with a white collar and cuffs trimmed in lace. The bodice had rows of tiny tucks, and several covered buttons adorned the neck. "Look how tiny the waist is! This was probably someone's wedding dress."

"Oh, Mom. It's red," Cindy said.

"Well, at the time this dress was worn, wedding dresses were always dark colors. Then, after the wedding, they could be worn for special occasions — a dress-up dress," Mom explained.

"Cindy, look at this." Jamie held up an ivory lace gown with a high neck and long full sleeves.

"Now *that's* a wedding dress!" Cindy said.

"That was your grandma's. It was especially designed for her," said Mom. "She wanted me to wear it when Dad and I married, but she was so much bigger than me! We never would have been able to alter it enough without ruining it."

Jamie stood up and held the gown against her. Grandma had been tall — like she was. The ruffle on the bottom even dragged on the floor. Maybe, Jamie thought, I'll be able to wear this someday. It's so beautiful! She folded it carefully and continued digging through the trunk, taking some comfort from the fact that other women in her family had been tall, too. Mom and Cindy might be petite, but she was just more like her dad and grandma.

"Something blue!" she said triumphantly, holding up a fragile, blue dressing gown.

"Well, lay it here and keep on looking," Cindy commanded.

Cindy's contribution, so far, had been to open trunk after trunk, look at what was lying on top, and if it wasn't blue she closed the lid and went on. She had advanced to writing her name and drawing a picture in the dust on top of each table, trunk, or box she passed.

"I'm all itchy," Mom said, wriggling. "It's certainly dirty up here."

Mom and Jamie continued to look through the contents of each box. Cindy finally wandered down to her bedroom, but she ran up and down the attic stairs every few minutes to check their progress.

"Cindy! I found it!" Mom yelled. She stood up, holding a light blue formal gown against her. The bodice glistened with a satiny glow. The neck scooped slightly and the sleeves puffed out along her arms. The skirt was long and full, with layers of soft, sheer ruffles that flowed over her jeans.

Jamie looked up. The tired mother that came home to them from the library every night had disappeared. In her place stood a soft-eyed, shiny-faced young woman.

Her mother held up a headpiece made of sparkling rhinestones. "Look, Cindy! Your crown — my old tiara." Mom placed it on her head and waltzed around. "My prom dress," her mother sang. She hummed an old song as she swayed from side to side.

Jamie realized her mouth was hanging open and hastily shut it. She could hardly believe that this vision wrapped in blue, dancing around the attic, was the same woman who yelled at her to clean up her room.

Even Cindy watched without interrupting.

Finally, Mom held the dress at arm's length before her and said, her eyes shiny with tears, "I wore this to the senior prom. Dad and I were crowned king and queen. That was the night we decided we couldn't wait any longer to get married. And the way things turned out, I'm glad we didn't wait."

"Mom, that's so romantic!" Jamie exclaimed.

"We got married just a few weeks later, in June, and moved in here with Grandma. We both worked all summer, then started at the university. It wasn't easy — living with Grandma.

"Anyway," she continued, taking the crown off and dropping the dress in a heap, "this is what we'll use to make your costume."

"We have some other blue stuff here," Jamie

said. She hated to have Mom cut up a dress that represented so many memories.

"No. This is perfect. There's plenty of fabric. It's in good condition. And . . . I want to use it."

Mom held it up against Cindy. "See how the color matches her eyes?"

Jamie had to admit it looked beautiful.

"C'mon then. We got the stuff. Let's get started!" Cindy grabbed the tiara off the floor and stuck it on her head. "I know I'll be the only one with a real queen's crown."

Mom folded everything carefully and put it back before gathering up the dress. She closed the lid, stroking it lovingly before starting after Cindy.

"Aren't you coming, Jamie?" Mom turned back when she reached the top of the stairs.

"Not yet. I think I'll look around a little more."

Jamie breathed in the dusty air surrounding her as she surveyed what she perceived to be a treasure trove. How could Mom just leave it lying around gathering dust?

As if she could read what Jamie was thinking, Mom said, "You know, I never realized exactly what was up here. There are some things we might consider moving downstairs. But we can't do it tonight, so don't stay up here too much longer. School tomorrow."

"I know, I know," Jamie muttered, squeezing

through boxes to get to the next chest.

She dusted off the top to get a better look at the carvings. "E . . . A . . . H? Must be initials. Whose initials?" she wondered aloud.

Jamie lifted the lid. Bits and pieces of blue and white filled her eyes. She reached in and took hold of the top layer, pulling it toward her. It was heavy for a piece of fabric. When she examined it more closely she discovered it was a quilt.

Jamie unfolded it completely. Rows and rows of fans appeared. Every fan was blue, but each piece that went together to form the fan was a different print. It was beautiful.

She turned up the bottom to look at the back and found the initials "E.A.S." embroidered in a corner.

Jamie folded the quilt and laid it aside to take downstairs with her. It was too wonderful to leave in a box.

She leaned forward to see what else was inside. She lifted out a second quilt. It reminded her of a flower garden. Each flower had a yellow center, surrounded by pastel print petals, surrounded by green hexagons, surrounded by white. She loved it, too! Jamie quickly flipped it over and found the same "E.A.S."

When she shook out the third quilt, she could hardly believe her eyes. "Mom! Mom! Come up here!" she yelled, all the while unfolding the quilt to see it better.

Her mother came running up the stairs. "What's wrong?" she said, breathing hard.

"Look! Just look at this!" Jamie held the quilt out for her to see.

"Oh! It's the house!"

"Here's my room. See?" Jamie pointed. "And yours and the living room, the dining room, the library, and the tower. Just look at the tower! It even has little yellow window seats."

"It's gorgeous." Her mother was, in Jamie's opinion, properly impressed. "Look at the fires in the fireplaces! And the furniture — it's so tiny, yet seems so real. That looks like the dining room table we're still using."

"I love it!" Jamie hugged it to her body. "I thought some of the others were great, but after I found this one. . . . You know, we ought to hang it up or something. Look at all the detail!" Jamie pointed to vases and lamps. "I see something new every time I look at it."

"Bring it down. We'll air it out, then think about hanging it up someplace," Mom said.

Jamie started to fold it, but decided to check the back of the quilt first.

"Look, it's signed like the rest of them are."

She held up a corner with "E.A.H." embroidered on it.

"Except the others said 'E.A.S.' I wonder if the same person did this one? The initials are the same as on the chest."

"Hmm? What do you mean?" Mom scooted closer.

"The quilts all have initials sewed on the back — by whoever made them, I guess. These two," Jamie said, pointing at the fan quilt and the flower-garden one, "have 'E.A.S.,' but this one has 'E.A.H.' and those are the same initials as on the lid of the chest."

"E.A.H.? Those are your great-grandmother's initials — Elizabeth Huddleston. The ones with 'E.A.S.' were probably made before she married your great-grandfather, George. They lived here during the thirties, the Depression, so that will give you some idea how old the quilts are."

Mom paused a moment. She shook her head. "Those were hard times," she said.

"Did you know them?" Jamie asked.

"No, not really. I may have met your great-grandmother once, but she died before Dad and I were married and your great-grandfather died many, many years ago. Dad didn't even know him."

"Dad told me all kinds of stories about his family, but I don't think he ever mentioned . . . who would this be? His grandfather?"

Mom nodded. "There were lots of tales about old George, but they weren't the happy, funny kind of stories your dad used to tell you."

"What do you mean?" Jamie asked, her curiosity rising.

"Oh you know — there are always rumors about old houses. . . ."

Jamie sat very quietly, giving her mom a chance to come up with the story.

Mom remained silent.

Jamie knew, even though she could barely restrain herself, that it wouldn't do a bit of good to ask her mother anything more about Great-Grandfather George. She would just have to find out some other way.

"We have these anyway," Jamie said, turning her attention back to the quilts. "And just think — my very own great-grandmother made them!"

She picked up the house quilt again. "This must have been how the house looked then. Isn't it great?" Jamie said.

"Yes, of course it is. But it's also late and you need a bath." Mom pulled dust balls out of Jamie's hair.

"I'll never be able to sleep tonight. This quilt, all that great furniture just sitting there . . . and a new job, too!" Jamie said.

"You'll sleep. You always do," Mom assured her, pointing toward the stairs.

"I was going to put this on my bed," Jamie said, wrinkling her nose, "but it doesn't smell very good."

Mom took the quilt. "I'll put it downstairs. You

can hang it out on the porch when you get home from school tomorrow."

Jamie held out her arms for the quilt.

"No," Mom said firmly. "A shower and bed."

"If you say so, sir." Jamie saluted smartly.

"But what about these others? Can I put one of them on my bed?"

She pointed at the fan quilt and the flower garden.

"They don't smell any better! Let's take them down one at a time," Mom said.

Jamie wasn't thrilled with the idea of leaving any of the quilts upstairs, but she stashed them back in the chest to keep in Mom's good graces.

"Mission accomplished," she said to Mom before turning on her heel and marching down the steps.

3

As Jamie rushed home from school the next day, she realized she couldn't remember even one thing they had discussed in any of her classes. All her thoughts had focused on working out a math lesson for Kevin.

She unlocked the door and stuffed her coat and books in the closet. Stepping into the living-room, she straightened pillows that were already straight and moved magazines off one table and onto another.

Jamie saw the quilt folded on a chair. She glanced at her watch and decided she had time for a quick look.

Jamie spread the quilt on the sofa. She was captured again by Elizabeth's handicraft. The materials and colors her great-grandmother had chosen blended together beautifully and the stitches holding it all together were so tiny, they were almost invisible. But most of all, Jamie decided, she was drawn by the warmth she felt flowing

27

from it. She stroked the tiny pieces of furniture, liking the differences in texture that the various fabrics provided. It was as if she knew each piece.

A sharp knock on the door tore her away from the quilt.

"Hi, Jamie." Kevin whirled around from looking at the street to greet her when she opened the door.

Jamie stood there awkwardly, holding the door open. "Come on in," she finally said.

Kevin staggered in carrying an armload of books and notebooks. He started to dump them on the sofa, but noticed the quilt just in time.

"Whoops, I sure don't want to mess that up." He looked around for a better place to put his books.

Jamie followed the path his eyes took about the room. She was struck by how many pieces of their furniture were frayed and shiny with wear. And the wallpaper had completely torn away from the walls in a couple of places. . . .

She turned to hide her embarrassment and walked briskly toward the kitchen. "It'll be easier to work in here on the table," she said brusquely.

Kevin readjusted his load and followed her. She pointed to a chair and he sat down, choosing one book out of the pile he had made on the floor.

"Where did you begin to have problems?" Jamie

decided to give a very businesslike tone to the session.

Kevin pointed to a page. "This is where I started falling behind and I've never caught up."

Jamie took the book and looked at the page he indicated. No wonder he's doing poorly, she thought. That chapter is basic to everything we've had.

Cindy burst in the front door then. "I'm home," she yelled.

"My little sister," Jamie explained, feeling the muscles in the back of her neck tighten. What would she blurt out this time?

"I'm hungry," Cindy yelled again.

"Just a minute," Jamie apologized, getting up to take care of Cindy.

"Come in here," Jamie called out to her sister, wondering if she would live to regret the move.

"Would you like something, too?" she asked Kevin.

"A Coke?" he asked.

Jamie yanked open the refrigerator door and took out two Cokes and an apple. She handed the apple to Cindy as soon as she walked in.

Cindy looked from Kevin to Jamie and back as she bit into the apple, turned, and started out of the kitchen.

Jamie rolled her shoulders a couple of times to

loosen them. Maybe Cindy wasn't going to pull one of her stunts this time after all.

Cindy stopped at the doorway.

Jamie's breath caught.

Cindy didn't say anything. She just looked over her shoulder at Kevin, then put her hand over her mouth and giggled.

Jamie felt her face grow hot.

"She's really cute," Kevin said.

Jamie just nodded, wondering if he was comparing her straight brown hair and brown eyes to Cindy's blue eyes and curly blond hair.

She set the Coke cans down hard and pushed Kevin's toward him.

"Let me explain how I work these problems, then you can do a few and we'll see exactly where you're having trouble," she said, wanting to get back to an area where she felt comfortable.

Jamie showed him her way of doing the problems, then asked him to work the first five.

While he was absorbed in figuring out the math, she took a good look at him, the way she had never been able to in school on the off-chance that someone would notice her interest in him. He really was a neat-looking guy, she thought, cataloging his attributes: dark hair, deep-blue eyes, long eyelashes, sparkling white teeth, and best of all, dimples!

Here I have a great chance to impress him, and

I don't know how! she thought a little desperately. She'd taken extra care with her clothes and hair that morning, but he probably hadn't noticed.

"I'm done," Kevin said, breaking in on her thoughts.

Jamie started and felt herself blush again. She hoped he hadn't noticed how she had been staring. "Let me check and see how you did."

He slid his paper toward her and she quickly checked it, easily focusing in on his weakness. He had made the same mistake in every problem.

Jamie pulled her chair around beside Kevin. "Look at this and this," she said, pointing to the same step on each problem. "You've put the y value in where the x value should be. If you remember x always stays to the left of the equal sign in these problems, you shouldn't have any trouble."

Kevin took the paper and studied it. Suddenly it was as if a light had gone on behind his eyes. He bent over and made some rough erasures, changing his answers. More sure of himself this time, Kevin handed Jamie the paper with a flourish.

She looked at each one and turned to her student, glowing with their success. "Try these," she said, pointing to the next set.

Kevin worked methodically and when finished, presented Jamie a perfect paper.

"You're a good teacher." Genuine admiration was in both his voice and eyes. "I've been trying to figure this out for weeks and you've explained it to me in just one hour."

Jamie wriggled in her chair, pleased with the praise, yet not sure how to respond to it. Finally, she smiled shyly and said nothing.

"You ought to do that more often," Kevin said.

"What?" Jamie asked, puzzled.

"Smile. You have a nice smile," Kevin told her.

Jamie willed the blush she felt growing to stop, but it was too late. She ducked her head.

Kevin shuffled his papers around. Jamie was aware he was doing it to ease her embarrassment.

He said, "Today is Thursday. Do you have any free time Saturday when we can get together again?"

"Sure, whenever you say," Jamie said.

"How about the afternoon? Say about one?"

"Okay. And before then, try to look over the next section and see if you have any questions. We'll start there."

Kevin slammed the book shut. "Thanks for the soda and the help." He smiled warmly. "Oh! If it's okay with you, my mom will just pay you once a week."

"Sure, fine." The mention of money reminded Jamie of why Kevin was there.

She walked with him to the living room.

"You know," Kevin said, stopping in front of her quilt. "I've never seen anything like this before. It's like a map or something."

Jamie was amazed that he even noticed the quilt.

"What's this?" he asked, pointing.

"It's the tower upstairs," Jamie explained. "You can see all around from it. There are windows on every wall, with window seats underneath where you can sit and look out or just lie around. It's my favorite place in the whole house."

Jamie relaxed as they began to talk about one of her favorite subjects. Her hair fell softly about her cheeks, which still felt slightly warm. She tossed it back over her shoulders when she looked up.

Kevin was staring at her as if he had never seen her before. Had she screwed up again by letting him see how excited she got over dumb things?

Kevin cleared his throat and looked quickly away. "Where'd you get this?"

"I found it in our attic with a whole bunch of other quilts and a lot of old furniture." Once again, in spite of herself, Jamie bubbled with the enthusiasm of her finds.

"You mean, like antiques?"

"I guess so," Jamie said, with a shrug of her shoulders. "They are things our family has had for years and years and just put upstairs when they became tired of them."

"Sounds great," Kevin said, looking interested.

"I'd really like to go up in your attic sometime."

"You would?"

"Yeah, I would."

"Why would you want to look at a lot of old stuff?" Jamie couldn't believe his interest was for real.

Kevin laughed. "My mom has a shop — an antiques shop. I'm constantly drafted to help her load and unload the furniture she buys when she goes to sales. To survive, I've had to develop an interest in it."

Jamie laughed with him. She couldn't believe her luck! He had to be the only boy in the world interested in antiques. And here he was with her in a house which had an attic full of them.

"Well, that will be your reward when you learn all your math, an all-expense-paid trip to our attic!"

"Sounds good to me!" He bent over the quilt again, then looked at his watch. "I'd better go. Your mom will be home soon, and so will mine. I've got lots of other homework to do besides math." He pointed to the stack of books he carried with him.

"See you Saturday," Jamie said as she watched him walk away.

And I won't blush the whole time, she vowed to herself. He wasn't even that hard to talk to, Jamie decided. If all she needed to get his attention was old furniture, she was set.

4

The fact that the sun was shining after a week of clouds and cold was a sure sign it was going to be a good day. Jamie was lying in bed, thinking, when Cindy jumped on her and pulled the blankets off.

"Get up, sleepyhead!" her little sister insisted. "Mom won't start working on my costume until you do."

"What time is it?" Jamie mumbled, rubbing her eyes.

"Time to get up!" Cindy said.

"Then get off me." Jamie sat up and Cindy tumbled off the bed laughing.

The smell of frying bacon encouraged Jamie to hurry. "Why is Mom making breakfast?" she asked.

"She said she was going to be working pretty hard and would need it," Cindy said.

Jamie stretched, then shuffled to the dresser to get her jeans and a favorite school sweatshirt.

"Hurry up!" Cindy urged once more before she

ran out of the room and clattered down the stairs.

Jamie plopped back on the bed for a minute. Kevin was coming again today. She looked down at the jeans and sweatshirt she had chosen and wondered if she should change into something nicer. Not now anyway, she decided. She'd just make sure she left plenty of time to clean up after she explored the attic.

"Jamie! Breakfast!" her mom called.

Jamie pulled on her clothes, then quickly brushed her hair and splashed water on her face.

"Smells goooood!" she said when she sat down at the table.

"Well, eat up. Once you get up in that attic, who knows when you'll ever get back down to eat again. I'm going to plant myself in front of the sewing machine, so you are on your own for food until supper."

The three of them dug in and polished off their breakfast.

"I'm so excited!" Cindy burst out. She jumped up and danced around the kitchen in a decent imitation of a fairy.

Jamie and Mom cleared off the table. "Leave the dishes," Mom said, stacking them in the sink. "I don't think Cindy could survive the wait."

Cindy led the way upstairs, still dancing. Mom disappeared into her bedroom and Jamie headed for the attic.

"The door is locked again," Jamie said, pulling at it. "Why do you keep it locked all the time?"

Mom tossed the key to her, then shrugged. "Want to keep all the skeletons locked tightly in their closet, I guess."

Jamie struggled with the lock and finally got it open. She flipped on the lights. Dust billowed all around, making her nose itch and eyes water. She went back for some rags.

"First order of business," Jamie mumbled to herself, "is to see if any of this furniture is the same as the stuff in the quilt. Then, I'll see how much of the other furniture is in good condition."

She attacked the piles of tables, chairs, desks, and trunks with dust cloths and energy, moving all the boxes against the wall and setting the furniture in the middle of the floor so she could see it better. Jamie lovingly cleaned each piece free of dust, then checked it for scratches, frays, cracks, or other signs of wear and tear. The pieces she thought might match those stitched in the quilt were sorted into one place, while other pieces were set aside in accordance with her plan to save the house. All Jamie had to do was move the beautiful antiques downstairs, and show Mom how great the house could look with just a little effort. She'd be so proud to have their house on the historical tour!

Jamie looked at the "other" pile. These pieces

would be the real life-savers. They could be sold.

Before she knew it, she heard Cindy call up the steps, "Oh, Jamie! Kevin's here!"

Jamie's stomach sank. She had completely lost track of time. She looked down at the streaks of dirt and grime on her clothes. And her hands were filthy. She was glad she couldn't see her face and hair. She heard footsteps on the stairs.

"Hi!" Kevin's head appeared. "Can I help with anything?"

"No!" Jamie said, rubbing frantically at the dirt spots on her clothes. "Just wait downstairs. I'll be there in a minute."

She at least needed to wash her hands and face and brush the cobwebs out of her hair. What had happened to the grand entrance she was going to make?

Kevin disappeared down the steps, giving Jamie a puzzled look over his shoulder.

Jamie ran down the stairs. She washed quickly and ran a brush through her hair. Catching a glimpse of herself in the mirror, she decided the clothes had to go. She ran to her room, dug through her drawers, and pulled out a clean pair of jeans and a sweater.

She took a deep breath, smoothed her hair and clothes, and walked slowly down the steps.

"Hi, Kevin," she greeted him casually, as though she hadn't brushed him off five minutes ago.

Kevin was bent over her quilt again. As she moved over to join him, she was almost overcome by the quilt's musty odor.

She gathered it up from under Kevin's nose. "Phew! I think I ought to hang this out to air."

Mom came in the room. "You'd better hang it in the back where the sun won't shine directly on it and fade the colors," she advised.

"I'll help," Kevin said, taking the quilt from Jamie.

They spread the quilt over the back railing of the porch. Kevin took one more good look at the "map" of the house.

"I'd really like to see your tower sometime," he said.

"We could work up there if you want," Jamie invited. "I usually study in the library — that's the room right here." She pointed it out to him on the quilt.

Kevin didn't answer. He continued to study the quilt.

Jamie waited, starting to regret the invitation. "It might be too cold," she said.

Kevin looked up quickly.

"No, I mean that's okay. I don't mind if it's a little cold. I really want to see it," he said.

They gathered everything they thought they might need and went upstairs. Jamie opened the door and motioned for Kevin to go ahead of her into the library. After he laid his books down, she led him up the short staircase to the tower. The sun had warmed the room to a comfortable temperature.

Kevin made a circuit of the windows.

"It's great. Your whole house is. It's so comfortable and warm, and it sounds corny, but homey or something," Kevin said.

Jamie smiled and nodded. He had summed up her feelings exactly, even if it was corny.

"We'd better get some work done," Jamie said, suddenly aware that Kevin was staring at her again in the same way he had the day before.

"Yeah, sure." Kevin took the stairs in a single leap, then plopped himself down at the desk in the library.

Jamie explained the next section to him and put him to work on some problems.

She went over to the sofa, sat down, and looked around the room.

The quilt, she recalled, showed the library very much like it was now, except for the desk. The small sofa was almost the same and the shelves were just as crammed with books. She marvelled at all the work — and patience — it must have taken to sew on all those tiny little books.

The desk that really belonged in here was still up in the attic. She had seen it that morning. It would look so much better than the banged-up, metal monster sitting there now.

Maybe she could set her plan in action by moving the desk down and putting the library back like it was in the quilt, Jamie thought. It wouldn't be too big a job. If she proceeded slowly, Mom wouldn't even realize what she was doing.

There were many pieces Jamie recognized on the quilt that she could move into other rooms. All of the second pile was old, old, old, and worth some money, Jamie hoped. She leaned forward and rested her elbows on her knees, her chin in her hands. There might even be something really valuable. Wouldn't that solve a few of their problems!

"What are you thinking about?" Kevin interrupted her reverie.

Jamie didn't know how to answer for a moment. She certainly didn't want to tell Kevin their financial woes.

"I was just wondering if a desk I saw in the attic this morning is the same as the one on the quilt," Jamie finally answered.

"Well, check my work here and we'll go see."

Jamie only had to glance at the answers to see that Kevin had improved in just two lessons.

"You're doing much better," she said. "You need to watch it when you have a problem like this though," Jamie pointed out. "You did this one right, but not this one. They're really the same if you look at them carefully."

Jamie wondered for a moment if Kevin had even been trying before. He was picking it up so quickly now.

But she couldn't help feeling a little glad for his math troubles.

"Look at it now," Kevin said.

Jamie checked the problems. She took Kevin's pencil and drew a big star at the top of the paper.

"I may have to frame it," Kevin said.

"Wait until you do as well on a test — where it counts," said Jamie.

"If I ever do."

"I think you will. A few more weeks under my instruction and you'll ace them all," Jamie said.

"What I want to know is, does this mean I get my reward?"

"What reward?"

"The tour of the attic!" Kevin reminded her.

"Oh, that! Sure, but first, I want to have another look at the quilt. I want to make sure I have the right desk."

Jamie went down the stairs first.

Barging into the kitchen, she stopped short. Her mom had a visitor. Jamie recognized him. It was Mr. Payne, the realtor, who was trying to talk her mom into selling the house.

"Hi, Jamie. How's the weather up there today?" Mr. Payne greeted her heartily. He was a scant five foot two to her five foot seven and always made it a point to make a joke about it.

"Hi, Mr. Payne," Jamie answered in a flat voice.

"You kids want a snack?" Mom asked.

"Not yet, thanks. We're checking something on the quilt."

"I'll get it," Kevin offered.

"Mr. Payne has someone interested in buying the house," Mom said.

"I thought you hadn't made up your mind yet," said Jamie.

"I haven't," Mom responded quickly.

"It's a wonderful offer for a house in this condition," insisted Mr. Payne.

"This house is in fine condition — all it needs is a little paint," Jamie said.

Mr. Payne looked at Mom and raised his eyebrows.

Kevin came in with the quilt and spread it on the kitchen counter.

Jamie turned her back on her mom and Mr. Payne and lightly smoothed the wrinkles out of the quilt.

"What an interesting old quilt," Payne said.

Jamie turned and found herself looking right

down on the top of the little man's head.

"And where did this come from?" he asked. "I don't remember seeing it before."

Jamie ignored the question.

"We found it in the attic a couple of days ago," Mom answered for her. "You'd never believe how much junk is up there."

"Oh?"

Jamie noticed Mr. Payne's eyes start to glow with interest. She threw Mom a warning look.

"I guess it's not really junk," Mom amended her statement. "A lot of people would call it antiques," she said with a shrug.

Jamie wished she could put her hand over Mom's mouth before she said anything else and got Mr. Payne interested in their furniture as well as their house.

"Antiques, you say. I know a little about antiques. I'd be glad to appraise your 'junk' for you, Mrs. Huddleston, and see if there's anything of any value," Payne offered.

Jamie frowned at Mom. She shook her head slightly.

"Maybe when we get this business with the house over and done with. I want to concentrate on one thing at a time," Mom said, her eyes meeting Jamie's.

Jamie relaxed slightly. Her mom had gotten the message.

"What's this made of anyway?" Payne turned back to the quilt and tried to take hold of the corner of it.

Jamie pulled it smoothly out of his grasp.

"Look at the rainbow shining into the tower," Jamie said to Kevin. "It's about to come loose." She ran her fingernail very carefully along the edges, smoothing the ragged seam.

"I know a quilt collector who would give just about anything for such an excellent example of the art as displayed here," Mr. Payne said, still trying to maneuver himself to get a good look at the quilt.

Jamie looked at Mom for help.

"Now, Emmett, you still have to convince me to sell the house," Mom said, "before you go on to the furnishings."

"Kevin, let's go check the desk. I'm almost sure it's the same one," Jamie said in a low voice.

"Let me put this out back first." Kevin went outside.

When he returned, Jamie hurried him out of the kitchen and up the stairs before Payne could suggest joining them.

"Jamie, what's with you?" Kevin asked as soon as they were out of earshot of the kitchen. "Is that guy your mom's boyfriend or something?"

The thought of Mr. Payne and her mother struck

45

Jamie as funny so she burst out laughing and had to sit down.

"Jamie? What now?"

Kevin's confusion got to Jamie. "Mr. Payne and Mom!" Jamie broke into laughter again.

"They *are* an unlikely couple." Kevin's mouth began to twitch. "I guess it is kind of silly to think of them like that."

"He's a realtor," Jamie explained, once she got control of herself. "He's trying to talk Mom into selling the house and I don't want her to do it." Telling Kevin about it sobered Jamie somewhat.

"He's one of those guys who always has a smart remark to make about everything — the remark you've heard two hundred times before. Like his 'how's the weather up there' comment. What a creep!"

"I'm glad he's not your mom's boyfriend," Kevin said, then smiled.

Jamie returned the smile, shaking her head. "That would be too much."

She stood up and began to wind her way through the attic to the desk. Kevin stayed close behind. Jamie finally stopped.

"What do you think?"

"It could be the same as the one in the quilt. But what about that one over there?" Kevin asked, pointing at a second desk.

Jamie compared the two desks, then moved back to the one she had originally picked.

"It's these round legs that make me think it's the one on the quilt," she explained, squatting down. "Most desks have square legs, don't they?" She looked at Kevin for confirmation.

"I guess so," he answered. "Other than that they are both the same style and the drawers are exactly alike."

He really looked at the quilt, Jamie thought. The drawers! She hadn't noticed the drawers.

"I'm going to ask Mom if I can move this one down," Jamie said, patting the desk with round legs. "It'll look perfect in the library. I want it to be just like on the quilt!"

Kevin looked all around him. "You know there are a lot of antiques up here. I've seen stuff like this around my mom's shop."

"Mom seems to think it's just junk, but I think it might be worth something."

"We've got a lot of books and pricing guides at home. I could bring some over next time," Kevin offered.

"Thanks, I'd like that," Jamie said.

Jamie sneezed several times. "I think that's about all of the dust I can take today," she said. "I hope you didn't get too dirty."

"It's okay — I've been lots dirtier. Why don't

we walk over to Al's and have a soda? If you've been up here most of the day, you probably need the walk to clear out your lungs."

Jamie looked at him. He was inviting her to go to Al's where everyone went and where someone might see them together? It was too much! The whole day had been too much.

"Sure, let me tell Mom," Jamie accepted casually, hoping she didn't have dust on her face or someplace else that would make her look ridiculous.

"Wait a minute!" Kevin called her back.

He was going to change his mind. Jamie knew it was too good to last.

"You have dust on the end of your nose." Kevin brushed it off.

Jamie got so flustered at his touch, she turned quickly and ran down the steps.

"I'll get my coat. Don't forget your books are in the library," Jamie called back to him as she floated down the stairs.

5

Jamie shut the door, then leaned against it, letting the smile she had been suppressing spread.

"Jamie? Is that you?" she heard her mother call.

"I'm home!" Jamie answered.

Mom came to the top of the steps and looked down at her standing against the door. "Anything wrong?" she asked.

"No. Everything is great."

"Okay," Mom answered, not sounding certain she believed her daughter.

Jamie took her coat off and threw it on a hook in the closet. She slumped in the recliner and relived the hour she'd just spent with Kevin.

She had felt so comfortable with him — not at all like she usually felt around boys. The conversation flowed! They talked about all the things she had found in the attic that morning. Kevin told her about some of the finds his mom had made at country auctions and yard sales. They discussed her mom's job at the library, their classes, and going to high school. And try as she might, Jamie couldn't remember even one time when she had blushed or stammered.

When Kevin brought her home he had said, "Let's meet after school Monday. I'll help you bring the desk down to the library, if your mom okays it, and then we can work on my math."

Life was glorious! Jamie couldn't remember a more perfect day.

"Why haven't you turned on any lights down here?"

Her mother's question roused Jamie to the fact that she was sitting in the dark.

"Oh, sorry." Jamie reached out and turned on the lamp by the chair.

"My formal is well on its way to fairyland," Mom said as she stretched out on the sofa across from Jamie.

"Good," Jamie answered absently.

"How is your job going?"

"What job?" Jamie looked at her mom, puzzled.

Mom shook her head. "Tu-tor-ing Kev-in."

Jamie looked at her blankly.

"That *is* why Kevin has been coming over?" Mom asked.

"Yes, of course," Jamie answered too quickly.

"Uh-huh," her mom said, chuckling.

Jamie searched frantically for some way to change the subject. She didn't want to talk to anyone about Kevin yet. She wanted to wait and see what, if anything, developed.

"Did anyone bring my quilt in?" Jamie finally settled on a safe ground for discussion.

"Forgot all about it," her mom mumbled with her eyes closed.

Jamie hoisted herself out of the chair and headed for the back porch. She flipped on the back lights and pushed open the door. There was nothing hanging on the railing.

Jamie rushed out to see if it had fallen on the ground. She leaned over the side of the porch and saw nothing but dirt and dead brown grass.

"Cindy!" Jamie turned to run inside and check if her sister had brought the quilt inside.

"Mom! Where's Cindy?" Jamie roused her mother from her half-dozing state.

"She went to Gail's right after you left. She's staying there for supper."

"Did she bring the quilt in?" Jamie asked, anxiety creeping into her question.

"No. I'm sure she didn't. Why?" Mom raised herself into a sitting position.

"It's gone!" Jamie said. She carefully lowered herself to the edge of the chair. "It's not out there."

"It has to be somewhere," Mom said, already on her way to the back door.

"No. It's gone."

Mom let the back door slam behind her. Jamie

got up and stood at the door watching Mom gallop down the steps to search the yard.

When Mom found no sign of the quilt, she came back in and led Jamie through a methodical search of the kitchen and living room.

"I know we didn't bring it in," she murmured barely loud enough for Jamie to hear.

"Someone took it. It's worth a lot of money — Kevin said so." Jamie spoke with certainty. She knew it was stolen. Why had she left it outside?

"C'mon, Jamie. Who would steal a quilt?"

"Mom, it's an antique. It's also signed and very special," Jamie explained earnestly.

"But no one would know that just seeing it hanging on the railing," Mom countered.

A sudden chill went through Jamie. By looking at her mom, she could tell she was feeling the same way. Someone had come into their very own yard, up on their own porch, and taken something that belonged to them.

Mom faced Jamie uncertainly. "Check upstairs just to make sure Cindy didn't bring it in."

Jamie ran up the steps and quickly checked all their rooms, finding nothing. She returned to the living room.

"Not there."

Mom stood there, looking at the floor, clasping and unclasping her hands.

Jamie waited for Mom to say something, do something.

"I'll call Cindy, just in case she put it somewhere we didn't see — or wrapped her doll in it for the walk over to Gail's — which is more likely."

Jamie watched her mom disappear into the hallway. She listened to her dial the phone and talk to Cindy, knowing somehow, all the while, that Cindy didn't have the quilt, that it was really and truly missing.

Mom stood in the doorway, between the hall and the living room and shook her head, then disappeared into the front hallway.

Jamie heard the lock on the front door click into place. She watched Mom hurry through to the kitchen and heard an almost identical click echo through the house from the lock on the back door.

Jamie began to gnaw nervously at her nails. When she looked up, Mom was pacing the hallway.

"We'd better call the police," Mom finally said, making her way to the phone a second time.

"Why?" Jamie asked, following her.

"Well, in case it shows up someplace. We need to have a report or something." Mom stood with her hand on the receiver.

Jamie moved closer to her mom.

Mom picked up the phone and dialed.

Jamie went to the back door and looked out

again just to make absolutely sure the quilt was gone. She felt horrible.

"They're sending someone over," Mom said. She put her arm around Jamie's waist. "Sorry I got so scared. I didn't mean to frighten you."

"I love that quilt," Jamie said.

"I know, honey."

"I was going to see how many pieces of furniture I could find and put them like they were in the quilt," Jamie said, still looking out at the empty porch railing. "I wanted to really fix up the house. . . ."

"Well, don't talk like we'll never see it again. Things do turn up," Mom replied, her shiny eyes and false smile betraying her words of optimism.

"Who would even want that quilt except us? Just think how Great-Grandmother Elizabeth would feel if she knew we lost it. Kevin liked it, too. He was going to help me find the furniture and move it down." All of a sudden, tears ran down Jamie's cheeks as she let all of her disappointment and fear pour out.

Mom left her arm around Jamie and let her cry.

A loud pounding on the front door startled Jamie so, her tears stopped. She felt Mom's arm tighten around her momentarily, then relax.

Mom reached up and wiped tears from Jamie's face.

"I'll get it," she said, moving away to the front

54

of the house. "Put some water on to heat. I need a cup of tea."

Jamie watched through the kitchen arch as Mom opened the door to a uniformed police officer.

"Good evening. I'm Officer Stephens. I understand you have a problem here?"

"Officer Stephens. Thank you so much for coming. Come in, please." Mom stepped back and invited him into the living room.

Stephens stepped inside and gave a quick glance around. He removed his hat and immediately a batch of dark curls fell across his forehead. He pushed them back impatiently.

"Someone stole our quilt," Mom blurted out.

Jamie observed Mom watching the handsome police officer who seemed to fill their living room.

"Was it taken from inside the house?" Stephens asked.

"No. It was hanging on the back porch, airing out. We just discovered it a couple of days ago in the attic. It's very old," Mom explained.

"Is anything else missing?"

"Not that I know of. I haven't really checked." Mom admitted with a slight quiver in her voice.

They should have checked to see if anything else was missing. Jamie chided herself for not thinking of it before.

She saw Officer Stephens take a form from the folder he had stuck under his arm. He sat down and began to write. Mom sat down across from him and tried to smooth her hair. Jamie knew she should go into the kitchen to put some water on, but she didn't want to miss anything, especially what seemed to be happening between Mom and the policeman.

"What time did you put the quilt out?" Stephens began.

"About three-thirty?" Mom looked at her for confirmation.

Jamie nodded.

"When did you discover it was missing?"

"Around five, when Jamie came home. It's sort of her quilt."

"Can you describe it for me?"

"Let Jamie do it. She can describe it better than I could."

Jamie stepped into the room.

"Is the water ready?" her mother asked her before Stephens could begin his questions.

Jamie shook her head.

"I'll take care of that if you'll help the officer."

Jamie nodded.

"Just give a brief description of the quilt. Anything distinguishing — color, size. . . ." Stephens smiled at Jamie, making her feel more at ease.

"It was definitely one of a kind," she began. "It was a fabric picture or map of our house. It showed the rooms and the furniture in each room. Each room was probably the color the room was when the quilt was made and the pieces of furniture were appliquéd in position. On the back it was signed 'E.A.H.,' the initials of my great-grand-mother."

Stephens listened carefully to Jamie's description, writing something on his pad from time to time.

Mom reappeared carrying a tray with cups of tea for all of them.

"We were just getting ready to have some tea. Maybe you would join us?" she said.

The officer nodded, smiling.

Jamie saw Mom had combed her hair and straightened her clothes while in the other room. She also realized that Officer Stephens had noticed it.

"Was anyone here during the time you think it was taken?" he continued.

"I was," Mom said.

"Did you hear anything? See anything?"

"I was upstairs, sewing. I didn't hear or see anything."

"Was anyone else here? Does anyone else live here with you?"

"Cindy. My youngest daughter. She wasn't home either."

"What about your husband?" Officer Stephens asked.

Mom shook her head. "I'm a widow," she said.

"Was anyone else around this afternoon?"

"Kevin Parker, a friend of mine," Jamie said. "And the realtor."

"Who?"

"Emmett Payne; he's a realtor," Jamie repeated.

Officer Stephens seemed to recognize the name. "Are you selling the house? Have people been coming through?"

"No, we're not selling," Jamie said. "Mr. Payne just wants us to sell it."

Mom cut in, "Mr. Payne appraised the house for me to help close my husband's estate. He contacted me because he has a client who is interested in buying the house. He stopped by today to pick up a key so he could have someone inspect the heating system and the roof."

Officer Stephens stopped writing and looked at Jamie and her mother. "Well, I have to tell you we've had a rash of antique thefts lately. There's a ready market for them today. We're beginning to suspect an organized ring is involved."

Jamie felt cold again. She took a gulp of tea to warm up her insides.

"This doesn't really fit in with the other reports." Officer Stephens shook his head. "They were real clean out jobs. A truck load at a time turns up missing."

Jamie looked into her tea cup.

Mom cleared her throat. "It's made us very nervous," she said. "I don't like the thought that we're so vulnerable."

"A common feeling after someone has had something stolen," Stephens assured them.

"We were wondering if you could watch the house a little more closely, just for a while?" Mom asked timidly.

"Be glad to," the officer said.

He was rewarded with huge smiles of relief from both Jamie and Mom.

"I'd like to check the area outside where the quilt was taken."

Jamie got up immediately and led the way to the back porch. "We put it back here so it wouldn't be in direct sunlight."

Stephens looked around the porch and the yard.

"Okay," he said, closing his folder and coming back on the porch. "We'll keep an eye out for it and also watch your house."

"Any chance we'll ever get it back?" Jamie asked.

Stephens looked at her and shook his head. "It's hard to tell. Anyone could have taken it from back here."

Jamie walked back to the living room with the officer trailing behind her.

"I'll check back with you in a few days," he said

to Jamie. "If you think of anything else, give me a call, all right?"

Jamie nodded, but all she could think of was that she might never see her quilt again.

"Thank you so much for coming over." Mom offered Stephens her hand.

He shook it gently. "My pleasure."

Her mother was blushing! It suddenly dawned on Jamie that perhaps it wasn't something that you outgrew.

As he was leaving, Officer Stephens checked the locks on their door. "Be sure you lock up whenever you're away or busy," he reminded them.

"Don't worry. I've already checked all the windows and doors at least twice," Mom said, then laughed nervously.

"Glad to see you have this deadbolt in addition to that old thing." The officer pointed to the ornate knob fixture that contained the original lock. "They open with skeleton keys — or it can be easily picked."

"We very seldom even bother to lock it," Mom said. "It's still there because it looks nice. But, I think I'll lock everything that has a key tonight."

Stephens nodded.

"Be careful," he said as he left, jamming the hat back down over his hair.

Mom shut and locked the door — both locks — after him, then busied herself with the tea tray.

"Nice man," Jamie began.

"Oh, yes," her mother answered.

"I feel better that he said they would watch the house," Jamie went on.

Mom continued to straighten the tray.

"He wasn't wearing a wedding ring," Jamie said, trying to get some response from her mom.

"Jamie! Really." Her mom disappeared into the kitchen before Jamie could say anything else.

Maybe this disaster with the quilt wouldn't turn out to be a total loss, Jamie thought with a smile.

6

Jamie dressed with special care for school on Monday, but it was the after-school tutoring session she had on her mind. She wore her red sweater and gray slacks. The red sweater, Jamie decided, brought out the highlights in her hair and made her cheeks look all rosy.

Kevin's greeting when he met her after school let her know it was worth it. "You look really great today," he said.

"Thank you," Jamie managed to say graciously.

"Are we going to move the desk first or are you going to make me do some math?" Kevin asked.

"Math, of course. Moving the desk is . . . another reward."

"I hope I won't be too tired," Kevin pretended to grumble.

Kevin and Jamie walked along in silence for a while.

"Oh my gosh! I almost forgot to tell you!" Jamie stopped in the middle of the sidewalk.

"What?"

"The quilt — it's missing!" Jamie announced.

"What do you mean . . . missing?"

"Saturday evening when I went to bring it in," Jamie paused dramatically and looked at Kevin, "it was gone."

"Did someone else bring it in?"

"No. It's really gone, missing, stolen. We called the police and everything," Jamie said.

"The police! You really think someone stole it?"

"I guess so. We feel so weird about it — you know, somebody taking it right off the porch." Jamie shivered.

"Who would have taken a quilt, for crying out loud?" Kevin said.

"Somebody who likes quilts. Somebody who knows what they're worth," said Jamie.

"That could be me," Kevin teased.

"Oh, Kevin, you aren't the kind of creepy person who would do something as low as taking a quilt off my own back porch."

"What kind of person am I?" Kevin asked.

Jamie felt really awkward.

Kevin didn't say anything else. He just took her free hand and squeezed it gently.

Jamie looked at Kevin and smiled shyly.

They walked the rest of the way home in silence.

Jamie led Kevin up the porch steps, taking care that he miss all the places that sagged.

"We're being very careful to lock everything now," Jamie explained as she searched through her backpack for the key they usually left in the mailbox. "That's what the police told us to do."

"Who came to check it out?" Kevin asked.

"His name was Stephens. He was really nice."

"I wondered if maybe it wasn't him. He coached our baseball team a couple of years ago. He's a great guy."

"Oh? Does he have kids our age?"

"No. As far as I know, he's never been married," Kevin told her.

That information made Jamie smile. She reflected once more on the possibility of Officer Stephens and her mom.

"What are you smiling about now?" Kevin asked, poking Jamie in the arm.

"I think he liked my mom," Jamie said.

Kevin shrugged. "Some guys like little, dainty, blonde ladies. I personally prefer — "

"Unlocked finally!" Jamie said, before he could go any further. She wasn't sure she wanted to hear what Kevin preferred. He'd already confused her enough by holding her hand most of the way home.

They pushed inside, juggling books and the heavy front door.

"You want something to drink or eat? I'm

changing my clothes before we go up to that filthy attic," Jamie said.

"Sure. I'll take a soda and anything you have to eat."

Jamie strolled into the kitchen to fix a snack.

"Where's Cindy?" Kevin asked.

"She has Brownies tonight. We can study uninterrupted for a while anyway." Jamie brought out two sodas and two bananas. "I thought half and half would be the best way to go," she said. "Half junk and half healthy."

"I'll eat anything. I'm a growing boy."

"Let's take it upstairs. We can work and eat at the same time. We'll get done sooner that way," Jamie said, already on her way up the stairs.

As soon as he set his food down in the library, Kevin bounded up the few steps to the tower.

"What are you doing?" Jamie asked.

Kevin was stretched out on one of the window seats. "These *are* comfortable." He ran his hand across the seat fabric and said, "You know, they're a different color than they were on the quilt and I like this much better. The gold material didn't match the room at all."

Jamie flopped down beside him. "They've been like this for as long as I can remember."

They sat quietly for a few minutes enjoying the view out the windows until Kevin finally said,

"We're not getting much accomplished up here, are we?"

"Nope," Jamie answered. "That desk will never get moved with us lounging around all day. You do the next set of problems and I'll go change my clothes."

Kevin was still working when Jamie returned. She started her own homework while he finished the assignment she had given him.

Jamie only found minor math errors when she corrected his paper.

"I may be too good a teacher," she said, handing his paper back. "I'm just about to do myself out of a job."

Kevin looked pleased. "I just wanted to make sure I didn't miss getting to move that big, heavy desk."

"You may wish you'd stayed with the math once we get up there," Jamie said.

They took the stairs to the attic two at a time. They had already moved the desk to the top of the staircase on Saturday. It wasn't hard to shift it around to carry it down the steps.

"I'll go first," Kevin said. "You lift your end enough to clear the steps . . . and be sure you don't go any faster than I'm going. I don't want to end up squashed."

Jamie got a firm hold underneath the desk. When she felt Kevin move down a step, she moved her end. She was glad it was a short flight. She wasn't sure how far she would be able to carry it. They certainly made furniture heavy in those days.

In a series of starts and stops they got the desk partway down when Jamie lost her grip and the desk shifted. The middle drawer banged against the wall.

Kevin leaned his end of the desk on the step and tried to reach around to close the drawer.

"I'll get it. It's my fault," Jamie said.

She stretched her arm around and under the desk. The drawer wouldn't budge.

"It's stuck. Do you think we can get it down this way?" Jamie asked, mad at herself for letting the desk slip.

Kevin looked over his shoulder. "We'll have to be careful, or we'll scratch the wall, but we can try."

They eased it the rest of the way down and into the hall with surprisingly little trouble.

Jamie leaned against the desk to catch her breath. She flexed her hands. They hurt from gripping the desk so tightly. She had a horrible feeling she would be very sore tomorrow. And they still had to get the desk into the library.

"Ready?" Kevin asked.

"Yeah." Jamie didn't want to waste her breath on talking until they were done.

She took hold of her end again. They carried it

a short distance and she had to set it down.

"Getting tired?" Kevin asked.

Jamie nodded. There was no sense in denying it.

"Me, too," Kevin said. "We can save some energy if we scoot it a little. Do you have some old rugs we can slip under the legs?"

"Sure, let me get them." Jamie ran down to the utility room to get some of the rugs they kept there to wipe their feet on.

She tiptoed back up the stairs, deciding to surprise Kevin. She reached the top of the steps and peeked around the corner.

Jamie creeped closer and closer, with Kevin still not hearing her. When she was close enough, she whispered, "What are you doing?"

Kevin's hand was deep inside the desk drawer that had opened on their way down the stairs.

"I'm trying to see what's making the drawer stick," he said, not in the least surprised.

"Here are the rugs." She threw them down beside the desk.

Kevin tugged at the middle drawer. "This is good and stuck. It won't open or shut. Something is caught way in the back."

Kevin jerked the drawer pull.

The desk creaked ominously.

"Kev, you'd better be a little more gentle," Jamie cautioned him.

He pulled on it again without success, then resorted to wiggling it in an attempt to force it open.

"You try," Kevin said finally, moving out of the way. "Your hand may be smaller than mine. I think there's a piece of paper along the back of the drawer that needs to come out."

Jamie felt around the drawer. She found the paper Kevin meant, but it didn't feel deep enough inside to be at the back. She worked the paper back and forth, trying to ease it out. Jamie made enough progress to be encouraged to keep trying.

"Is it coming?" Kevin asked.

Jamie shushed him. She didn't want any distractions. She tried to see inside the drawer.

"Kevin, it isn't stuck in the back at all." Jamie tried to keep her rising excitement under control.

She reached back in and tried to manipulate the paper. She pulled the drawer out a little more. The wood shrieked in protest.

"Look!" Jamie pointed at what she had found.

The wooden drawer bottom was slipping back, uncovering a stack of old papers and another bottom.

"It's a false bottom!" Jamie said, thrilled with the discovery.

Kevin started to reach in to take out the papers.

"Kevin?"

"What?"

"Do you think I could look at what's in there first?"

Kevin looked a little sheepish. "I guess it is your desk," he said, stepping aside.

Jamie pushed the false bottom back as far as it would go, then carefully removed the papers. They were yellowed with age and covered with ink scrawls faded to a dull brown.

"What is it?" Kevin asked.

Jamie could tell by his voice he could barely control his curiosity. She thumbed through the stack slowly.

"What are you doing, for Pete's sake? Just tell me what they are," he said again, more agitated.

"It's letters," Jamie said simply.

"Who are they from? Who are they to? What do they say?" Kevin asked.

Jamie squinted to try and make out what the top letter said. She moved into the library with Kevin dogging her every step.

She sat down at the metal desk and turned on the light. Kevin took up a seat on the corner of the desk.

"They are dated in the thirties. See?" Jamie pointed to the date scrawled in the upper corner of the top letter. Kevin leaned over to get a better look.

"It says, 'Dear Elizabeth.' Kevin, I'll bet it's the

same Elizabeth who made my quilt!"

Jamie read on.

"This one is about trying to get money together to save the house. It must have been during the Depression. It says, 'I am working day and night to save the house and get us back together again. I never knew how important it was to me until I almost lost it. I hope you are doing well. I miss you more than you could possibly know, but you are much better off at Aunt Nell's. I only light the stove during the evening after I get home from work until I go to bed. I pile on many quilts and pray it doesn't get too cold during the night. That's no way for a lady to have to live.'

"Kevin, I know just how he feels. Mom wants to sell the house, you know, and we are cutting corners right and left. We only turn the furnace up after school until we go to bed — just like he says." Jamie bent over the letters again.

"They *are* to my Elizabeth. See? It's signed 'George.' Mom said she was married to a George. Maybe these letters will tell me what it was that Mom didn't want to tell me about him."

The sound of a key turning in the lock downstairs distracted Jamie from her reading.

"Kevin, what time is it? Is that Mom already?"

"It's four-thirty," he said, looking at his watch.

Jamie got up and went to the top of the stairs. She was more than a little surprised when she saw it was Mr. Payne who was already halfway up the staircase.

7

"Why, Jamie! I knocked and didn't get an answer so I thought no one was home," Mr. Payne said.

"I didn't hear any knock."

"Maybe you were sleeping too soundly," he joked.

"I wasn't sleeping at all. I was . . ." Jamie's voice trailed off.

The letters! If Mr. Payne came upstairs he was bound to see them. And Jamie didn't want him to. He'd stuck his nose into too many parts of her family's life already.

"What are you doing here anyway?" Jamie asked.

"I was going to take a look at the antiques in your attic. I talked to your mother about it earlier today."

"And she agreed?" Jamie felt a flutter of irritation with her mother.

Mr. Payne nodded. "She said if no one was here I should use my key."

Jamie wondered if she should call to check out

73

his story with her mom, but knowing Mom, she probably did agree. Jamie reluctantly stepped out of his way.

"What have we here?" Payne asked, immediately taking in the desk. His walk speeded up as he moved toward it.

Jamie hurriedly slipped around him and tried to get the drawer shut before he saw the bottom.

Mr. Payne somehow managed to get up to the desk before she could get the drawer closed.

"It's just a false bottom," Jamie said quickly. "We found it because it was making the drawer stick." She pushed the drawer shut, almost catching the realtor's fingers.

He pulled them out quickly, blowing on them.

"Was there anything in it?" Payne asked.

The question, asked so innocently, caught Jamie off guard. She hemmed and hawed, trying to think of something to say.

"No, it was empty," she said, but she knew she'd waited too long to answer and given away the fact they had found something.

Payne walked around the desk, seeming to examine it.

"I've always been very interested in this house, ever since I was a little boy and heard those stories," he said mysteriously. "I never really believed there was money hidden somewhere," Mr.

Payne let drop, "but who knows? You've found a good place to hide something."

Mr. Payne stopped and leaned down, peering under the desk.

"What do you think?" he asked Jamie, catching her off guard again.

"I don't have the slightest idea what you're talking about," she said firmly. "I thought you wanted to look at the furniture."

"I do, I do. You want to come along and show me what else you've found?" Payne asked.

"The attic is that way." Jamie pointed her thumb over her shoulder and headed back to the library.

Kevin was poring over the letters when Jamie joined him.

"That man is here again," said Jamie, seething with anger.

"Huh?" Kevin looked up at her.

"Mr. Payne. The realtor you met Saturday. He says he's supposed to look at the antiques and tell Mom what they're worth. He saw the desk with the drawer hanging out and he's suspicious."

"Suspicious about what? You get a little carried away when it comes to Mr. Payne. I asked my mom if she knew him when I got home on Saturday, because the name sounded familiar. She said she bought stuff from him all the time. He travels around buying antiques quite a bit, so he really does know something about them. You just don't like him because he wants your mom to sell the house. I can't blame you — it's a great house."

"Have you read all of the letters yet?" Jamie said, annoyed that he would stick up for Payne.

Kevin laid them down. "No, not all of them."

"Well? What do they say?"

"Not too much. Just about the hard times and how much he misses his family."

"Well, I want to keep them between us — sort of a secret — for now," Jamie gathered up the papers and swept them into the desk.

"Who would I tell?"

Jamie chewed the inside of her cheek, thinking. "Sorry," she said shortly. "I want to read them first, before Mom. She'd probably give them to Mr. Payne to sell."

Kevin burst out laughing.

"Why are you laughing?" Jamie demanded.

"This thing you have against Mr. Payne. Don't ever let *me* get on your bad side!"

"You'd better keep up with your math then," Jamie said.

Kevin held up his hand. "I promise," he said.

"You're right about Mr. Payne. I am being un-reasonable," Jamie admitted. "But I just have to convince my mom that selling the house isn't the solution to our problems. Maybe I can use these letters about how hard my dad's family worked to keep the house when times were hard.

"I guess Mr. Payne is just tending to business — even if that means minding everybody else's, too."

Kevin reached over and ruffled her hair.

Jamie pushed his hand away, but smiled.

"Getting back to our 'secret letters' — what did you read?" Jamie asked again.

"He mentions the quilt."

"He does? Where?" Jamie pulled the letters out again so Kevin could show her.

He rustled through them for a few minutes, then pointed to a passage that Jamie immediately devoured.

"I got the house quilt today. When I think how hard you worked to piece that together, I know you share my belief that it is worth all the trouble it is causing. I hope you will not be too upset when you see the small addition I made to it — a little something for a rainy day. You have shared the bad times and I want to make certain you have the opportunity to share the good."

"That's strange," she said, looking up from the letter. "What do you suppose he added to the quilt? Do you have any ideas about what he might mean?" Jamie asked Kevin, perplexed.

"No, but it makes me want to see the quilt again. We could probably tell from the stitches what he added," Kevin answered.

"No such luck." Jamie shook her head sadly.

Someone pounded on the door below.

"Who is that now?" Jamie said. "Put these someplace while I go see who it is. Don't let *you-know-who* see them." She pointed toward the attic.

When Jamie opened the door, she was surprised to see Officer Stephens standing there with his hat in his hand.

"Well hi," she greeted him.

"Hi, yourself. How are things going? Anything missing today?" Stephens said.

"No. Nothing." Jamie just stood there for a few minutes, wondering what she should do. "Do you want to come in?" she finally asked.

"Sure." Officer Stephens stepped into the hall-way. "Is your mom home?"

"She's still at work."

Officer Stephens glanced around the hallway. "When will she get back?"

"She's usually home by five," Jamie said.

"Okay. I'll try to stop back by then."

"Have you found out something about my quilt?" asked Jamie.

"No, not yet. Just thought I'd ask your mom a few more questions."

"Sure. She won't mind."

Jamie heard Mr. Payne coming downstairs from the attic. She turned to see him wave to Officer Stephens.

"Dan, how're you doing?" Mr. Payne greeted the police officer.

"Great, Mr. Payne. Just great."

"Jamie, tell your mother I'll get in touch with her about those items in the attic," Payne said.

"I'll be sure to do that," Jamie said.

"Tell your mom I'll talk to her later, too," Officer Stephens added.

"I will." Jamie herded the two of them toward the front door and gave a sigh of relief when they were outside.

She ran up the stairs to the library.

"Who was it?" Kevin asked, looking up from the letters.

"Officer Stephens. Mr. Payne left, too. He didn't spend much time in the attic."

"No, he stopped here on his way out."

"Did he see the letters?"

"He saw them, but I said it was just homework," said Kevin.

"Darn!" Jamie fumed. "Do you think he believed you? Did he say anything else?"

"About what?"

"About the hidden money!"

"Jamie, when you start talking about Payne you

don't make any sense," Kevin said.

"Oh, that's right. You weren't there when he was talking about it. He said he'd heard stories about this house since he was a little boy. Have you ever heard anything?"

Kevin shook his head.

"It's probably one of those rumors that Mom says goes along with a big, old house," Jamie said. "Did you find out anything else about George from the letters?"

"Not really. He was having money problems and he hated banks," Kevin said.

"I'll read them all later," Jamie said, gathering up the letters again and looking around for a place to put them. "I hate to put them back in the drawer. Mr. Payne knows about it."

"Jamie, I don't think you have to worry about that. He doesn't have to sneak around to get what he wants. Your mom would show him anything he wanted to see."

"You're right — and that's another reason not to tell Mom about them just yet," Jamie said.

She went into the hall and placed them in the drawer, pulling the false bottom back in place. "Let's get this moved."

They placed the rugs under the legs of the desk and scooted it into the library.

While Jamie positioned the old desk as she remembered it on the quilt, Kevin quickly slid the other desk into Cindy's room.

"What do you think?" Jamie asked, when Kevin returned.

"Looks right to me. I just wish we had the quilt to look at again."

"You and me both," Jamie said.

Kevin rubbed his hands together. "Anything else, Chief?" he asked.

"Not that I can think of. I need to get supper started. Mom will be home anytime now," Jamie said.

"When should we work again? I don't want to tie up all your afternoons," said Kevin.

"It's okay with me. I mean, whenever it's convenient for you. I have to come home to take care of Cindy anyway. If you want a lesson you can come anytime."

"I'll talk to you at school tomorrow, then."

Jamie walked him to the door. "It bothers me not to be able to figure out what George added to the quilt."

"All we can do is try to remember anything unusual. It'll come to us out of the blue," Kevin said.

"Hope so. I'll see you tomorrow."

"Goodnight," Kevin said, turning and waving at the end of the walk.

Jamie headed back to the library. She wanted to read the letters for herself.

She was halfway up the stairs when the front door opened, and cold air filled the stairway.

"Jamie! Hi!" Mom called up to her.

Jamie turned around and came back down. "Mom, I don't have dinner ready."

"What have you been doing all afternoon?" Mom asked, but not at all like Jamie expected. She didn't sound mad.

"Kevin came over. We worked on his math, then moved the desk I was telling you about out of the attic. Then Mr. Payne showed up, and Mom, he didn't even knock when he came in. He just used his key and walked right in. Then, Officer Stephens came by to ask you more questions . . ." Jamie's voice trailed off. A lot had happened that afternoon.

"No wonder you forgot about dinner! We'll fix a snack sort of supper. You're probably tired anyway. Dan caught me at the library before I left."

"Dan? Who's that?" Jamie asked.

"Officer Stephens."

"Oh," Jamie said.

Mom gave her a half grin.

"You're not mad that I didn't get supper ready?"

"No," Mom answered.

"Did Mr. Payne call you or anything about the furniture?"

"As a matter of fact he did. He thinks we have some solid pieces up in the attic. He said there wasn't anything special or particularly valuable, but we could make a tidy sum if we decided to sell them. And if we're moving from this house, we certainly won't have anyplace to keep them."

"What do you mean, if we're moving?"

"I didn't mean to blurt it out like that," Mom said. She spoke very slowly. "I mean that Mr. Payne has received a formal offer on the house."

Jamie swallowed hard. "Does that mean you've decided to sell?" She felt like someone had hit her in the stomach. *Her* house!

"Jamie, I have to consider it." She turned and faced Jamie, the laughter in her eyes fading.

"I know you don't want to move, but we may have to and now that we have an offer . . . it seems like a good time." Mom's voice had a pleading note in it.

When Jamie didn't answer, her mom added, "The offer is so good. I can't believe someone would pay that much for all the trouble this house will give them."

Jamie knew her mom wanted to say, 'Isn't that wonderful! We'll be so happy someplace else!' But she couldn't.

"Why don't we sell the furniture and use the money to fix up the house?" Jamie suggested.

"Jamie, we wouldn't get *that* much!"

"Have someone else look at the furniture. Mr. Payne didn't even stay that long. He couldn't know how much everything was worth."

Mom laughed. "That's what Mr. Payne said you'd say. Did you have anyone in particular in mind?"

"No. Why?"

"Not even Kevin's mother?"

"I never even thought of Kevin's mom. I just think it would be better to have more than one opinion."

"Well, we'll see. You go on upstairs and get your homework done. I'll fix supper."

"Mom, you can't sell the house. It's my house! It's our home . . ." Jamie was close to tears.

"I have until Wednesday to decide. That's a couple of days, so we can talk about it later. You need to think about it some more with your head and not your heart."

Jamie opened her mouth.

"I'm too tired to listen to you now," Mom said firmly.

From her tone, Jamie knew better than to pursue it any further. She had a couple of days. She would do just what Mom told her to do — use her head. Except she planned to do that to bring Mom around to her point of view.

Jamie trudged up the steps. She started for her room, then decided to study at the "new" desk. Might as well break it in.

Once she sat down, homework was the last thing on Jamie's mind. She rubbed her hands over the desk, feeling all the scratches and nicks. Jamie took out the letters and looked for the one about the quilt.

Darn it anyway! She had forgotten to ask her mom about what Mr. Payne had meant when he told her there were stories about the house.

Jamie pushed back her chair and ran downstairs.

"Mom!" she called out.

"What?" Mom answered from the kitchen.

"Mr. Payne said something that's been bothering me," Jamie said.

"Honey, Mr. Payne can't say anything without it bothering you."

"But this was different. He said he'd heard stories about hidden money in our house. What did he mean?"

"Oh, Jamie, there are always stories about old families that live in old houses."

"Is there one about our house? I'd like to hear it if there is."

Mom sat down on the high stool beside the kitchen counter.

"As a matter of fact there is a story about money hidden in this house, but it's just that. It has to do with Great-Grandfather George, the one we were talking about the other night."

Jamie swallowed the feeling of satisfaction she had at her mother's words — she knew it involved her great-grandfather somehow. "Why didn't you tell me then?"

"Well, it's not a very happy story . . . and you're the one who is always saying how wonderful this house is, but you don't know or never think about the bad things about it. It almost ruined your great-grandfather during the Depression.

"The bank here in town failed. Your great-grandfather lost a lot of money. He had the house mortgaged to the hilt and was in danger of losing it, too. Somehow, he talked the bank into giving him extra time to get the money together to pay off the loan.

"He sent Great-Grandma off to stay with his sister and then set about working himself half to death."

Mom paused and took a breath.

"That doesn't sound too weird. Things like that happened everyday then, didn't they?"

"They did, but that's not the whole story. Give me a chance to get it straight. It changed your great-grandfather. All he did after that was work, work, work. He continued to run his business — the feed store — but he was seen in other places at all hours of the day and night. Nobody seemed to know what he was doing, and he wouldn't answer any questions. So people made up their own explanations."

"Like what?" Jamie interrupted.

"Like he was doing all kinds of things that were illegal — smuggling, spying, bootlegging. You name it and someone claimed they saw him doing it.

"Then one day, he walked into the bank and paid off the loan in one lump sum, in gold. Nobody knew where he'd gotten that much money, although everyone had their own ideas."

"He paid off the loan, so people thought he was a crook?"

"People didn't have money like that in those days. Plus he was acting suspiciously — coming and going at odd hours, turning up where no one expected him," Mom said.

"But what about the rest? What about there being money hidden someplace?"

"That got started because people figured if he was doing something illegal and made enough money to pay off the bank, he probably made more. And then he died. He caught a cold, it turned into pneumonia, and he died. After all that work, he didn't even get to enjoy the house."

Poor Great-Grandfather, Jamie thought. But she couldn't help feeling a little excited — money hidden somewhere in their very own house!

"I believe if there was any money, someone in the family would have found it by now," Mom said.

"You've got to admit, it's kind of fun to think about," Jamie said.

"Don't let your imagination run away with you," Mom warned. "Just get upstairs and concentrate on your homework. I want to eat soon."

Jamie returned upstairs in a much better mood. This was her kind of story.

She went up to the tower, sat on the window-seat, and tried to imagine where the money could be. The secret drawer in the desk would be the perfect place to hide money, but all that was in there were letters.

She thought about the way the house must have been then — when her great-grandfather had lived in it. Jamie closed her eyes and tried to visualize it.

Her eyes flew open. She jumped up and rushed down the steps.

Jamie rummaged around in the drawers of the desk until she found a paper and pencil.

Laboriously, she tried to draw what she could remember about the quilt. Her nose almost touched the paper and her knuckles were white from clenching the pencil.

After a while, she straightened, then tried to rub the tiredness from her eyes.

Jamie leaned back and looked at her drawing.

She shook her head. "I never was much of an artist," she said.

Mom stuck her head in the door. "What did you say?"

Jamie hastily turned the paper over. "Thinking out loud," she said.

"Cindy's home and dinner is ready. Homework done?"

"Not quite," Jamie answered.

"Hey, that desk looks nice there! Did you move the other one into Cindy's room?"

Jamie nodded.

"Find any other good stuff?" Mom asked.

Jamie shook her head, letting her hair cover her face. She felt bad not telling Mom about the letters.

"Well, you can eat now or I'll just leave it out for you to eat later. It's just some sandwiches."

"I'll be down in a minute."

As soon as she was sure Mom was out of the way, Jamie took the drawing out again.

8

"Jamie, why aren't you up yet?" Mom came to the door of Jamie's room.

"My throat is a little sore this morning." Jamie was still in bed with the covers up to her neck. She made sure her voice came out croaky.

Mom walked over and put her hand on her daughter's head. "You feel a little warm. Open up."

Jamie opened her mouth wide and stuck her tongue out.

"I can't really tell anything. I don't know why I always do that," Mom said.

"My head hurts, too," Jamie admitted a little reluctantly.

"I guess I can take a day off from work and stay here with you."

"Mom, I'm not a baby. I can stay here by myself. I probably have a little virus. If I can just rest for a day or two, I'll be fine."

"I hate to leave you here with no one to take care of you."

"But I don't want to be taken care of. I just want to rest." Jamie made herself sound fussy.

"I'll come home at lunch time and check on you. If you aren't feeling any better, I'll make an appointment for you with the doctor," Mom compromised.

Jamie just buried herself deeper under the covers and tried to look miserable.

Mom stood up. "Let me get Cindy off and then I'll be back with some aspirin."

Jamie closed her eyes.

It wasn't long before her mother had her settled to her satisfaction and left for work only a little later than usual.

As soon as she was sure the coast was clear, Jamie got up, dressed in old jeans and a shirt, and made her way to the tower room. She opened the curtains to the winter sun. Looking out the windows, she saw not a cracked sidewalk and weed-infested lawn, but masses of flowers and the smooth carpet of grass she had planned for the summer.

A dart of fear pierced her daydream. She might not be here when summer came. She might be in a dinky apartment somewhere.

Jamie shook it off. She didn't feel all that well, but she wasn't as sick as she had made Mom think she was. She just wanted a chance to have some time to herself, a chance to figure out how to save the house.

Jamie took her quilt picture and the letters out of their hiding place in the library and carried them back to the tower, settling comfortably on one of the window seats. She still hadn't had a chance to read them all the way through yet.

As she looked at the picture she had drawn, Jamie knew it was trying to tell her something, but she couldn't understand what.

She put the drawing aside and spread the letters out before her, looking for something in one of them that might give her a clue to the truth about her great-grandfather. Jamie flipped through them until she found the one about the quilt. She started reading it from the beginning:

Dear Elizabeth,

Quite soon, I am certain, we will be back together. The house is safe — at last. I don't know how much longer I could have stood the strain.

I surprised the whole town the other night by going to that new moving picture — *The Wizard of Oz*. It was almost what I would call inspiring. Something had been bothering me for a while, and I didn't know quite how to tell you. Now I think I've found the perfect way.

The young girl who played Dorothy reminded me of our little Tressie, except Dorothy could sing and we both know Tressie can't carry a tune. The best song in the movie was about rainbows.

The Wizard of Oz is one of my favorite movies! Jamie thought. And here is my great-grandfather talking about how it was when it first came out.

Jamie skimmed the part about the quilt she had read earlier.

The letter ended:

Dorothy had some words of wisdom for us. She said, THERE'S NO PLACE LIKE HOME. Be sure to remember that. You can go over the rainbow, but the best things are right here, with a rainbow above them.

Jamie's head snapped up. Someone was knocking on the door. She crawled over to the window and peeked out. It was Mr. Payne!

She heard the scrape of a key in the lock.

He must think no one's at home, she realized.

Jamie gathered up the letters. She didn't want Payne to see them. And she didn't want to see Mr. Payne.

If she could make it to her room and stay very quiet, he might not know she was there.

Jamie started down the steps to the library.

"Hallo! Anybody home?" Mr. Payne said as he opened the door.

He was already inside. If she came out of the library to go to her room now, he would see her as she walked by the stairs.

Jamie listened to his footsteps. She could tell he was going through the downstairs rooms one by one.

She heard Mr. Payne start up the steps. When he reached the second floor, she expected to hear him go up to the attic, but instead she heard him start down the hallway toward the library!

Jamie's eyes flew about the room searching for a place to hide.

Her eyes finally rested on the window seats — the perfect place! When Jamie and Cindy were younger, inside the seats was their favorite place to hide when they played hide and seek.

As fast as she could, and still keep quiet, Jamie crossed the room. She lifted the lid on the nearest seat and crawled inside. As she slowly closed it, she felt her watch catch on the ruffle.

Jamie pulled gently, but it wouldn't come loose! She pulled again — still nothing. She gave a mighty tug and heard the seat fabric rip. No time to worry about that now. She only hoped Payne didn't hear it.

Jamie held her breath as she listened to Mr.

Payne's steps getting louder and louder and finally stopping.

She heard the scratch of the top drawer as he opened the desk in the library. Jamie clutched the letters to her chest, glad she had had the foresight to carry them with her.

Jamie heard him open the other drawers one by one — then silence.

Suddenly the sound of his movements was drowned out by a heavy pounding from down-stairs.

The pounding stopped, then resumed.

"Jamie! Jamie! Are you there?"

It was Kevin. What was he doing there? Why wasn't he in school?

Oh, no, if she heard him from inside the window seat, Mr. Payne must hear him, too.

The front door hit against the wall. Mr. Payne must have left it unlocked, Jamie thought, and Kevin was coming in.

"Jamie? Are you up there?" Kevin was at the foot of the stairs calling out to her.

Jamie couldn't hear Mr. Payne moving about anywhere. Maybe he was going to stay where he was and hope Kevin left.

Kevin started up the steps.

Jamie tried to think of some way to signal Kevin.

She heard him hesitate at the top of the stair-case.

Jamie knew she couldn't let him walk straight into Mr. Payne's arms. She threw the window seat lid open, crawled out, and moved quietly to the steps.

"Mr. Payne!" Jamie heard Kevin say.

"Kevin," Mr. Payne answered in his most polite tone.

"Where's Jamie?" Kevin asked.

"At school, I would imagine."

"I'm right here, Kevin," Jamie said, moving into full view.

"There must be something wrong with the acoustics up here, Jamie," Mr. Payne said. "This is the second time you've failed to hear me knock."

"I'm sick," Jamie said with as much dignity as she could muster.

"Is it your ears?" Payne asked.

"What are you doing here?" she asked him.

"Taking another look at the furniture," said Mr. Payne.

"Really? Did you talk to Mom? If you had, she would have surely told you about me being home."

"There were just a few things I wanted to check again before I gave her a report."

"She told me you already reported to her," said Jamie.

Mr. Payne shook his head and gave a short laugh. "That was just a preliminary report. I still need to do a formal inventory and appraisal."

"And Mom asked you to do this?" Jamie asked.

"Jamie," Kevin interrupted.

Jamie and Mr. Payne both turned toward Kevin, who had been standing in the doorway of the office silently during the entire exchange.

"I talked to my mom last night about the furniture. She said she'd be glad to look at it for you, too."

Jamie rubbed her forehead. That was the worst thing Kevin could have said.

"I'm sure she would," Mr. Payne said to Kevin, then turning to Jamie, "You can be assured I'll be more than fair with your mother. I know where I can get top dollar for your antiques," he boasted.

"We don't even know if we want to sell them!" Jamie protested.

"I think that's your mother's decision. She won't have much room for them anyway after she sells the house."

Jamie's head began to really pound.

"And what's he doing here?" Mr. Payne pointed an accusing finger at Kevin.

"I don't know," Jamie said. She sank down to the bottom step. "Maybe he wants another look at the furniture, too. It seems to be very popular."

The three of them stayed as they were for a while, no one saying anything.

"If you were going to inventory the furniture," Jamie began and slowly raised her eyes until she was looking directly at Mr. Payne, "what are you doing in here?"

Payne cleared his throat. "I decided to start with this desk," he explained.

It didn't convince Jamie at all.

"I think you'd better come back later when my mom is here," she said.

Mr. Payne walked slowly to the door. "Tell your mother if she is interested in any of this, she'll have to see me," he said to Kevin as a parting shot.

Jamie and Kevin remained where they were until the front door closed.

"That man!" Jamie burst out. "I told you he wouldn't be satisfied with just getting the house — now he wants the furniture, too!"

"Jamie, calm down." Kevin tried to soothe her. "There are some good pieces of furniture. I checked in the guides. He is a businessman, after all."

Jamie stood up. "Kevin, what are you doing here? Shouldn't you be at school?"

"I'm missing a study hall, that's all," Kevin said. "I wanted to make sure you were all right."

Kevin reached over and lifted Jamie's chin.

"Are you?" he asked.

Jamie sighed. "I'm okay. I have a little headache, but mostly I just wanted to stay home and try to think some things out. Mom is getting serious about selling the house."

She finally managed a smile for Kevin. "It was sweet of you to come check on me."

"I wanted to."

Kevin's smile convinced Jamie what he said was true.

"Thank goodness that noseybody's gone," Jamie said. She ran up the steps to the tower.

Kevin followed.

Jamie looked out the windows and saw no sign of Mr. Payne or his car.

"What's with the rip in the seat?" Kevin asked, pointing at the window seat cover.

"I caught my watch. I hope Mom won't be too mad," Jamie said.

"How'd you do that?"

Jamie demonstrated how she'd opened the lid and climbed inside, catching her watch.

"Wow! That's a great place to hide, but why'd you do it?" Kevin wanted to know.

Jamie shrugged. "I just didn't feel up to talking to Mr. Payne, that's all. And then he didn't go to the attic at all. Kevin, don't you think that's strange?"

The phone rang.

"Uh-oh. I'll bet that's my mom," Jamie said.

She ran and answered the extension in the upstairs hall.

"Jamie, how do you feel?" Mom asked.

"I'm doing OK," Jamie said. She put her fingers

over her lips to make sure Kevin kept quiet.

"Mr. Payne called me and said he might stop by to look at the furniture again."

"He's already been here, Mom. Kevin is here, too," Jamie confessed. It would be better for her mom to hear it from her rather than Mr. Payne.

"What is Kevin doing there?"

"He just stopped by to see if I was all right. Mom, Mr. Payne just walked in again. You have to get that key back."

"Jamie, you are trying to change the subject. I want you back in bed and Kevin back in school," Mom ordered.

"Yes, Mother," Jamie promised and hung up the phone.

"You have to go," she said to Kevin.

"I'm already late. You think you'll be better tomorrow?"

Jamie nodded.

"I want you to come to my mom's shop and see some of her books and stuff," Kevin invited.

"I'd like to do that," Jamie said. "Does she have any quilts?"

"Only a whole roomful."

Kevin moved to the top of the stairs, then turned back. He took her hand and squeezed it, then was gone before Jamie could say or do anything.

Her head was pounding. Why did Kevin have to be so nice? Jamie wondered. He just made her like him more and more. Jamie knew she should go to bed, but she decided she would take the quilt picture and the letters with her.

Jamie reached in the window seat and immediately located the bundle of letters. When she drew them out, the quilt picture wasn't with them. She reached in again and felt all around, but found nothing.

Jamie finally lifted the lid and stuck her head inside to see. Nothing!

She let the lid slam down and hurried to the desk. Jamie pulled open drawer after drawer, finding no sign of her picture. She dropped to the floor and crawled around on her hands and knees looking for it. No luck. It must have fallen into a crack or behind something. She'd have to start all over again — after her nap.

9

"You didn't happen to see the picture I drew of my quilt yesterday, did you?" Jamie asked Kevin as they walked to his mother's shop the next afternoon after school.

"No, I don't remember it. I really didn't look at much of anything except Mr. Payne . . . and you," Kevin said.

"I had it out looking at it before Payne showed up, but I couldn't find it after you left. Oh well, I'll run across it sometime."

"Here we are," announced Kevin.

He stopped in front of a tiny storefront with a red and navy striped awning over the doorway and the one big window that faced the street. Kevin opened the shop door and let Jamie go in first.

Jamie paused inside the doorway, her eyes jumping from one object of furniture to the next, all grouped here and there about the room in organized disarray.

"Mom!" Kevin called out.

A tall, dark-haired woman stepped from behind a gingham curtain hanging over a doorway to one side of the room. She strode toward Jamie and Kevin.

Kevin took Jamie's hand and pulled her toward the woman.

"Mom, this is Jamie. Jame, this is my mom."

Jamie held out her free hand. "I'm pleased to meet you, Mrs. Parker. What lovely things you have here."

It was difficult for Jamie to pull her eyes away from the displays and concentrate on being polite to Kevin's mom.

Mrs. Parker took the hand Jamie offered. She looked her over carefully.

"So you're the young lady we've been hearing so much about! You must be very special, as much as Kevin talks about you. Not to mention the fact that you're the only one in eight years of school who has been able to give him the slightest glimmer of insight into math."

Kevin shifted uncomfortably when Jamie looked at him.

"Anyway, we thank you for what you've done." Mrs. Parker patted Jamie's hand. "Kevin says you're interested in quilts."

"I found some quilts in our attic. One of them was . . . very special. I guess you could say I have an interest in them," Jamie finally got out.

"Come on back and I'll show you what I have."

Mrs. Parker led the way through an open archway into a small back room.

Jamie realized the outside of the shop was deceiving. There were any number of small, connected rooms wandering around the interior of the store, making it much larger than it seemed at first.

Jamie's eyes traveled along one wall. "Oh!" she gasped.

Her eyes moved around the corner of that wall to the next.

She pulled her hand away from Kevin's and clasped both her hands under her chin. She gasped again.

Jamie came to a third wall. "Beautiful," she murmured.

"It's almost like looking through a kaleidoscope. There are so many patterns and colors," she said to Mrs. Parker.

"I'm so glad you like them — and appreciate them!"

Jamie walked over to the far wall. She reached toward one of the quilts, then pulled her hand back quickly.

"May I touch?" she asked.

"They really make you want to reach out and stroke them, don't they?" Mrs. Parker said.

Jamie agreed.

"I don't encourage touching, but this once I guess it will be all right."

Jamie reached out and ran her fingertips lightly over a quilt that looked very much like the fan quilt she had found in her attic, except each fan was made up of both different patterns and colors.

"I have one like this, except it's all blue and white," Jamie said.

"You're the second person today to display an interest in that fan quilt," said Mrs. Parker. "In fact, the other person was someone you know, your friend, Mr. Payne."

Jamie groaned. "He's no friend of mine."

Mrs. Parker smiled and looked over at Kevin. "He came in to see how he should price a quilt like that one," Mrs. Parker explained.

"He said he had one?" Jamie asked.

"He said he had a chance to get one, but he wasn't too knowledgeable about quilts and didn't know how much to offer the seller."

"It better not be *my* fan quilt he's talking about," Jamie said, frowning.

"I told him I'd be willing to take it off his hands," said Mrs. Parker. "And he said he didn't know if he was going to bother with it. He might just stick with furniture. I must say, he certainly is very good when it comes to that. Whenever I have a client who has a special request, I always call

Emmett first. He's reliable and he's reasonable."

Kevin mouthed, "I told you so," to Jamie.

"I'll bring my quilts over sometime and let you see them," Jamie said.

"I'd like that, dear," Mrs. Parker answered. She put her arm across Jamie's shoulders. "I have a couple of books picked out, if you'd like to read a little more about quilts."

"Oh, yes," said Jamie.

"I wonder though" — Jamie looked around at the quilts again — "how can you sell them? How can you bear to let someone carry them out of here?"

Mrs. Parker laughed. "I hardly can! Sometimes, I just decide I'm not going to sell one or another — unless it's an offer I just can't say no to. After all, I keep reminding myself, I am in the business of selling."

Jamie laughed with her.

"Jame, if we're going to get any studying done, we'd better go," Kevin reminded her, pointing at his watch.

"Thanks for showing me these," Jamie said to Mrs. Parker.

"Anytime — I was anxious to meet Kevin's friend."

Mrs. Parker handed Jamie several books on their way out.

Jamie stopped at the counter and started to thumb through one of them.

"You can look at that while I'm studying," Kevin said right into her ear.

Jamie snapped the book shut and linked her arm with Kevin's.

"Let's go," she said.

"See you later, Mom," Kevin said.

"Thanks, Mrs. Parker," Jamie added.

"Don't be too late, Kevin," Mrs. Parker called after them.

10

Jamie and Kevin walked much faster than their usual pace toward Jamie's house.

In the middle of the block, Jamie stopped.

"Darn, I almost forgot. I have one more errand," Jamie said.

"Do you mind?" she turned to Kevin and asked.

"What is it?"

"I need to stop by Mr. Payne's office and get the key to our house. Mom finally agreed to ask for it back and I told her I would stop by for it today."

"Does that mean she isn't going to sell the house?"

"She's talking with somebody at the bank today about it. She decided she needed some 'guidance' or something before she could make an 'informed decision.' I think she wants to sell it, but wants someone to tell her she's doing the right thing. I'm certainly not going to be the one."

"I guess we could stop and get it. It'll only take

a few minutes and if we don't, he'll only walk in and interrupt us again."

"A few minutes is all I can take of the man," said Jamie.

They turned at the next corner and were at Payne's real estate office.

Jamie pushed open the door and entered.

An older woman, wearing some of the heaviest eye makeup Jamie had ever seen, looked up from the book she was reading when Jamie and Kevin entered.

"What can I do for you kids?" she asked in a slightly gravelly voice.

"Can I see Mr. Payne, please?" Jamie requested.

"Not here," the woman answered shortly and looked back down at her book.

Jamie cleared her throat. "Then maybe you can help me," she said.

The woman looked up again, her eyebrows drawn almost into a straight line by her frown.

"What?" she demanded.

"I'm supposed to pick up the key to our house from Mr. Payne. Huddleston, thirteen-seventy-two Monroe."

Without getting up, the receptionist rolled her chair backward and stretched to look at a peg board hanging to one side of her desk.

"It's not here. Maybe that's where he is, taking

the key back to your house or showing it."

Jamie tried to hold back her sigh of disgust. "Thanks," she said.

Out on the sidewalk, Jamie looked up and down the street.

"He'd better not be there again," she said to Kevin.

They turned back the way they had come.

"I think we can cut through behind this building and get to your house faster," Kevin suggested, pointing at a narrow alley between Payne's office and the next building.

"You certainly are anxious to get to work on your math," Jamie said, surprised.

"I'm finally starting to understand it a little," Kevin admitted, "and I don't want to lose the momentum."

"What teacher could ask for more?" Jamie said, going down the alley after him.

"And who could ask for a better . . . or prettier teacher?"

Jamie kept her eyes on the ground. Kevin had thrown her off balance again with his compliment and made her more determined to be what he seemed to see her as.

Behind Payne's office, a dilapidated garage at first seemed to block their way. Kevin went around to the far side to see if there was room to get through.

Jamie went up to the garage and pressed her face against a window. She rubbed a circle of dust away and pressed her face against it again.

Jamie could hardly open her eyes wide enough to take in the sight before her. Furniture was stacked against every wall almost to the rafters.

"Kevin!" she called without taking her face away from the window.

"We can get through on the other side," she heard him say.

"Come here first. I want you to see all this stuff," she said.

Jamie moved aside so Kevin could take a look.

"So he's into antiques," Kevin said pulling back. "We knew that."

"I want to go in," Jamie said.

"You can't do that!"

"I want to see what's in there," Jamie repeated, more forcefully this time.

"That's no different from Mr. Payne coming into your house. In fact, it's worse. He at least had a key. If we go in there, it will be breaking and entering."

"I know," Jamie said, frustrated.

"Unless it's unlocked," Kevin added.

Jamie moved swiftly to the front doors. A hinged latch, secured by a lock, held the two doors together, but the lock hung open. She couldn't believe her luck! Someone had goofed.

She removed the lock, folded the latch back, and pulled the doors open only wide enough to step inside. Once in, she leaned out and hung the lock back on the hook and motioned for Kevin to follow her.

Jamie darted back inside. Kevin stayed in the doorway, taking an occasional peek out of the crack between the two big doors.

As soon as she made a complete circuit of the room, Jamie rejoined Kevin.

"What did you see?" he asked.

"Do you think he bought all this?"

"I would imagine so. That's part of his business." Kevin looked around the room. "He certainly is a busy man."

"Why is it all just laying around here?" Jamie asked. "Why doesn't he have it in a shop somewhere? What good is it doing him here?"

"He doesn't have a shop. He sells to shops," Kevin tried to explain.

"Then why is there so much? Where did he get it all? Your mom says she tells him what she wants and he goes out and finds it. That's different than having all this stuff laying around here."

"Maybe he's getting ready to open a shop. I don't know. Let's just get out of here."

Jamie could tell Kevin was losing patience with her. She looked around once again.

The sudden roar of a truck engine alerted Jamie to the danger of their position. She looked at Kevin. He placed his finger over his lips, then looked out the door.

He pulled the door tightly shut, grabbed Jamie's wrist, and pulled her toward the back of the garage.

"What is it?" Jamie hissed.

"A truck — backing into the alley. There's no place for it to go but here."

Jamie's stomach rumbled. She thought it must be the fear she felt swelling in the hollow of it. She was too weak to move. Kevin kept pulling her.

"The window!" He pointed toward it.

Jamie willed her feet to move in that direction.

Kevin pushed the window upward. His face turned red and the cords in his neck stood out. The window creaked slightly, but didn't move.

"Is it locked?" Jamie whispered, trying to get herself under control.

Kevin shook his head and wiped his forehead on his coat sleeve.

"It feels like it might come open with just a little more. . . ."

He ran his fingers around the edges of the window. "It's all this dirt making it stick."

Jamie watched Kevin work with the window.

A rumble and screech right outside the door signaled the truck had come to a stop and their time was up.

Jamie searched frantically for a place to hide. She heard a car pull up outside and stop. The car door opened, then slammed. Footsteps crunched on the gravel.

Her search became more desperate. A large, old wardrobe caught her eye. If only it was empty! This time Jamie dragged Kevin.

When they got to the wardrobe, she grabbed the handle and pulled. It wouldn't open.

Jamie wiped her hands on her jeans and pulled again. With what seemed like an earth-shaking screech, the door flew open and Jamie almost fell backward.

She regained her balance and climbed inside, waiting for Kevin to follow.

He scrambled in and pulled the door shut, leaving them in total darkness without an inch to spare.

The stench of mildew surrounded them. Jamie almost gagged, then found herself feeling short of breath. There wasn't enough air. They would suffocate in there.

She grabbed Kevin's arm and dug her fingers in tightly. Kevin patted her hand. Then they heard a voice.

"Did anyone see you?"

Jamie stiffened and clutched Kevin's arm even more tightly. It was Mr. Payne!

Payne spoke again. "Leave the truck here until tonight. We'll make up a full load out of this and what we got today and get it out of town."

"What else should I load?" an unfamiliar voice asked.

Jamie heard Payne moving around the room. A knock here and a grunt there made it through the walls of the wardrobe.

Payne's footsteps became louder.

Jamie wished she could see Kevin.

The wardrobe shook slightly from a blow against the side where Jamie was crouched.

She stuffed her knuckles into her mouth and bit down to keep from crying out.

"That should just about make a load," Payne said. He sounded like he was talking right to them, he was so close.

"And don't go off and leave the lock open this time," Jamie heard Payne say angrily.

Two sets of footsteps faded as the men moved away from the wardrobe.

The truck roared to life. The motor sputtered and died. The engine fired up again. Jamie heard the gears groan and felt the vibrations of the truck moving closer and closer to the wardrobe.

The wardrobe rocked gently when the bumper

nudged their hiding place. In spite of the cold, she felt perspiration trickling down her collar.

The roar of the engine was abruptly silenced, the door of the truck opened. Someone moved toward them.

A man groaned, then cursed as he tried to shift the wardrobe.

"I can't load that thing by myself," she heard the driver mutter. "It's going to take two people."

Jamie felt the kick he aimed at the wardrobe.

Don't let it fall, please, don't let it fall, she prayed silently.

The wardrobe stabilized.

Jamie wanted to let out the breath she had been holding, but was afraid the man might hear.

In horror, she listened to the creak of the garage doors as they swung shut with a clang. The lock clicked sharply and footsteps on gravel faded slowly.

They were locked in!

11

Silence settled over the garage. The smell of exhaust overpowered that of mildew.

"Jamie, are you okay?" she heard Kevin whisper.

Jamie nodded, then realized he couldn't see her any better than she could see him.

"Jamie?" Kevin reached out and touched her face.

"I'm okay," she said.

Jamie pushed his hand down.

"We're locked in," she said.

She heard Kevin let out a long breath.

"Do you think we should get out of the wardrobe? What if they come back?" Jamie whispered.

"They said tonight. I heard them leave and lock the door. We'd better get out while we can."

Kevin pushed the door open slightly and put his eye to the crack he made. He pushed the door a little farther, then Jamie felt him shift.

"Great — the truck has us blocked in," he said.

"I don't know if I can get out or not."

"Take off your coat."

Kevin's elbow, then his shoulder poked Jamie in his struggle to get out of his coat. He shifted again.

"I don't fit," he said. "You try."

Jamie and Kevin squeezed past one another as they changed positions. Jamie tried to get her coat off. Kevin finally reached over and helped her.

"You know you're one of the few boys in junior high that's bigger than me and I get stuck in a closet with you!" Jamie said to Kevin.

"Can you get out?"

Jamie put one leg out the door and took a deep breath. Carefully she squeezed out the small opening.

"Now get me out," Kevin said.

"How?" Jamie asked, looking around the garage for possibilities.

"Just get in the truck and drive it through the doors. That would solve both of our problems," Kevin suggested.

"I can't do that!"

"Well, you think of something."

Jamie pushed on the back of the truck, but it didn't even rock.

"I'll have to go get help," Jamie said, wondering how she was going to explain it.

"NO!" sputtered Kevin. "Get in the truck, push

in on the clutch, shift it into neutral, and see if it will roll forward any. It just has to move a little."

"I don't know anything about driving!" Jamie protested.

"Then it's time to learn."

Jamie went around to the door on the driver's side. She pulled herself up the step and looked inside. There were all kinds of pedals and gear shifts and levers. She didn't know what to do.

"The clutch is the floor pedal that is farthest left. The brake is next to it. You'll need to know that so you don't go through the door.

"The truck will be in neutral when the gear shift is loose. Just kind of knock it out of whatever gear it's in after you push in on the clutch," Kevin continued.

Jamie opened the door to the cab and climbed in. She stared at the floor pedals and finally pushed in on the one she thought was the clutch. She smacked the gear shift lever, hoping that would knock it into neutral. It didn't move at all.

She grasped the gear shift and found it already moved loosely.

"I think it's in neutral," she leaned out and said to Kevin. "But nothing is happening."

"Take the emergency brake off."

Jamie searched for what might be a brake lever. Right under the dashboard on her left, she found a lever that said "Emergency." She took hold of it with sweaty hands. Jamie turned it slightly and it released.

The truck rolled forward. Jamie slammed her foot down on the brake as the garage doors loomed closer.

She removed her foot from the clutch pedal and pushed down hard on the emergency brake.

Jamie slid off the seat to the floor.

"Thanks."

Jamie looked up and saw Kevin standing over her.

"Don't ever ask me to do anything like that again," she said. "Look." Jamie held out her hand. It was shaking.

"We'd better get out," Kevin said.

When she was sure her legs would support her, Jamie got up and walked to the back of the truck. She pushed up the back door. It opened easily.

"What are you doing now?" Kevin demanded.

"I want to see what's in here." Jamie started to climb up on the bumper.

Kevin put his hands on Jamie's waist and tried to pull her down.

Jamie squirmed and wriggled until she freed herself and pulled herself back up inside the truck where Kevin couldn't reach her. It took a moment for her eyes to adjust to the dimmer light conditions.

"Omigosh! Omigosh!" she exclaimed over and over.

Jamie went farther inside and knelt before a chest. She felt along the top carefully. She knew even before she found the initials what it was. Her fingers traced the grooves in the lid — E. A. H.

"What is it?" Kevin asked as he climbed into the truck.

Jamie pushed him out backwards, then jumped down and slammed the door shut.

"I can't believe it," she said, shaking her head. "We've got to get out of here. We've got to call the police."

"Why?"

When she didn't answer, Kevin took Jamie by the shoulders and shook her. "Why?"

"The furniture in the truck . . ." Jamie took a deep breath. "It's from my house!"

12

"We can't get out. We're locked in," Kevin reminded her.

"We have to. Go try the window again."

All Jamie could think about was that she had to get to Mom before she did anything about the house.

Kevin pushed on the window, changed position, and pushed again. It let out a creak now and then, but it didn't move even a fraction of an inch.

"Let's just break it," he finally said, breathing heavily.

"No!" Jamie said. "They'll know someone has been here."

"Then you try." Kevin moved away from the window.

Jamie examined the window carefully. There was no lock, so it was something else that was keeping it shut. It was filthy dirty for one thing. She reached around for her backpack and rummaged around in it until she found a fingernail file.

Bit by bit, she pried dirt from the tracks of the window frame.

After clearing one side, Jamie switched to the second. Immediately, she discovered what was keeping the window from opening.

"It's nailed shut," she pointed out to Kevin. "We need a hammer to get the nail out."

"A hammer? Do you have one in your pocket by any chance?" Kevin asked.

"Yeah, sure," Jamie said sarcastically. "There's got to be one around here. Look in the truck."

Jamie turned back to the window and grasped the nail, trying to wiggle it loose. It wouldn't budge.

"Kevin? Find anything?" she called over her shoulder.

He appeared carrying a hammer head, but no handle. "They don't take very good care of their tools around here."

Jamie grabbed the hammer head and grasped the head of the nail with the claw end. She gently rocked the head and in a short time held up the nail triumphantly for Kevin to see.

Jamie pushed up on the window and it slowly raised. She wiggled through and jumped to the ground.

In a moment, Kevin landed beside her.

"My house," she said. "We can call from there."

They ran forward, but Jamie pulled up short after a few feet. "I left my backpack."

"You can get it later."

"No, they might come back and see it. They'd know someone was on to them and get away."

"They might get away anyway," Kevin reminded her.

Jamie turned and went back to the garage. She pulled herself up over the sill, and went back inside.

When Jamie returned, her backpack was slung over her shoulder.

"What took so long?" Kevin wanted to know.

"Tell you later," Jamie said.

13

They reached Jamie's house.

"See? I'm dirtier than I was in your attic," Kevin said, trying to brush the worst of the dust off.

"You can do that later. C'mon."

Jamie put the key in the lock and tried to turn it. "He didn't even lock the door when he was through," she said in disgust, pushing it open.

Kevin headed straight for the phone.

"Make sure you talk to Officer Stephens," Jamie said to Kevin.

"I think we should tell whoever answers."

"Think for a minute. We're two kids who are reporting that a respected citizen has a garage full of stolen antiques that we found when we broke in. Someone who knows us will give us the benefit of the doubt; somebody else may not."

"Officer Stephens, please," Kevin said as soon as he got an answer.

"When do you expect him back?" Kevin listened to the voice on the other end.

"Okay, leave a message for him to call Kevin Parker at 555-0290."

He hung up the phone.

"Not there, but they expect him back any minute and he'll call us."

"What should we do now?" Jamie asked. "I'm too charged up just to sit here."

"Shouldn't we tell someone else since we can't get hold of Dan?"

Jamie shook her head so hard her hair covered her face. "We'll have too much to explain to anyone else. They said it would only be a few minutes."

"What about your mom? Shouldn't we call her?"

"Yes!" Jamie grabbed the phone. "We have to call her. She can't sign that contract to sell the house."

"What was I thinking about," Jamie mumbled as she punched out the library number.

"Mom?" She practically shouted when a voice answered.

"This is Jamie," she said more quietly. "May I speak to my mom, please?"

"Where is she? I need to talk to her now."

"If she does come back, have her call me immediately. It's an emergency."

Jamie slammed the phone down and started pacing.

"She isn't there. She told them to tell me if I called that Cindy is at Lynn's and she has some business to take care of this evening so she'll be late. Oh, Kevin, I hope she isn't signing those papers to sell the house!"

"Just try to be calm."

Kevin put his arm around Jamie and tried to lead her into the living room.

Jamie pulled away. "Upstairs. Let's go upstairs to the tower."

Jamie went straight to the windows and looked out. When she sat down on the window seat, she discovered the spot she had ripped the day before. She ran her fingers over it.

"I forgot to tell Mom about this," she said.

Jamie pulled the edges of the rip together, then folded back the corner. She kneeled in front of the bench and ran her hand over the covering again.

"This is so lumpy." She ran her hand over the top of the padding a few more times, then reached under the seat cover.

When Jamie turned around to face Kevin, she had something cupped in her hands.

"Jamie? What is it?" Kevin asked, walking toward her.

Jamie held out her hands. "Money. There's money in here!" she said.

"Money?" Kevin repeated.

She looked down at what she had pulled from underneath the cushion. Gold coins glittered in her palms.

"Jamie, that's not just money, that's gold," Kevin said, his voice full of wonder.

Jamie turned back around and laid them on the cushion, then pushed her hand under the cushion again. She came out with another handful.

"The rainbow and the pot of gold — that's what he added to the quilt!" Jamie burst out, "but I forgot about it."

"What? What are you talking about?"

"In the letter. Great-Grandfather said he added something to the quilt. It must have been the rainbow. That's what the gold on the window seats meant, too. He was marking where he'd hidden the coins. He did everything but say it in the letter when he talked about the song from *The Wizard of Oz* — something about the best things are right here with a rainbow above them. But I forgot to put the rainbow on my drawing of the quilt! And it fits in with what my mom told me the other night."

"What did your mom tell you?" Kevin asked.

Jamie gathered the gold coins in both hands and carried them down to the library. When she let them trickle through her fingers, they sounded almost musical.

"Kevin, come help me count them," she said, looking up at him standing on the steps.

But he wasn't paying any attention to her. His eyes were glued to the door of the library. Jamie followed his gaze.

She could barely hold back a scream when she saw Mr. Payne standing there, a grin creasing his face from ear to ear.

"What are you doing here? My mom hasn't sold you the house yet," Jamie said. She stood and started toward him.

Payne put his arm out and blocked the way.

"I'm calling the police!" Jamie said.

"I don't think so," Mr. Payne answered.

"We found your little hideaway, Payne — and all your antiques." Kevin stepped behind Jamie and put his hands on her shoulders.

"What hideaway? What antiques?" Payne asked in a pleasant voice.

"Behind your office. We were there this afternoon when you brought in your latest load."

"But that's just an empty storage shed! Or it will be by the time you get back there."

"When we tell them what we found . . ." Jamie started.

"You think they'll believe you? You'd do anything, say anything, to block the sale of this house. And that's just what this feeble story about me stealing all of your antiques is — an attempt to keep your mom from selling this house. When your mother finds out that the house was broken into again, she'll be so anxious to get rid of it. . . ." Payne's smile grew.

But Jamie had him now. "How did you know our house was broken into? I didn't say anything about that. Nobody knows except me, Kevin . . . and whoever did the breaking in."

Out of the corner of her eye, Jamie saw Kevin move stealthily toward Payne.

"Kevin, won't the police be delighted when they find out where some of those stolen antiques are that they've been trying to track down? It's just such a shame that they're going to find some of them in your mother's delightful little shop."

Kevin stopped. "If there's anything in there that's stolen, she got it from you."

"Never, never." Mr. Payne shook his head.

"Kevin, he wouldn't dare sell stuff he'd stolen from around here to shops in this area," Jamie said, trying to call Payne's bluff.

"Must I say it again? I didn't sell them to her. I just happen to have some information that would lead to the irrevocable conclusion that they are, unfortunately, stolen." Payne let out a sigh. "It would put her out of business, ruin her reputation, Kevin, whether it's true or not."

Kevin folded his arms across his chest, his face flushed.

"They'll believe us," Jamie insisted, trying to convince both Kevin and Payne.

"And if they don't? Jamie, dear, I want you to gather the coins for me and put them in here." He held out a bag to her.

"I wouldn't want to compound your troubles by leaving you with this tainted money in your possession," Payne said smoothly.

"Tainted? Who are you to talk about tainted? The coins are mine!"

"Why did your great-grandfather go to all the trouble of hiding them so carefully if there wasn't something wrong with them? Nobody really knows where or how he got that money . . . except me," Payne said smugly.

"That's ridiculous! My great-grandfather wouldn't do anything wrong. He was just trying to save this house," Jamie contested.

"An unfortunate trait that seems to run in the family," Payne said.

Payne's tone changed abruptly. "Now do what I say. I don't have time for chitchat."

"What did you come back for?" Jamie asked, trying to stall for time.

"The coins, of course. It seems we both solved the mystery at the same time."

Tears of anger and frustration burned Jamie's eyes, but she wasn't about to let Payne see her cry.

"I must possess a little more curiosity than you," Mr. Payne continued. "I dug deeper than you did — and discovered that your great-grandfather had a weakness for hiding things in secret drawers in desks." Payne withdrew an old, battered book from his pocket. "George's ledger," Payne said. "I found this little treasure in the bottom drawer of his *other* desk — in a *second* false bottom drawer."

Jamie snatched the book from Payne's outstretched hand.

"As you can see," he sneered, "George had quite a bit of money that was unaccounted for. I was confused at first by the rainbows penciled in next to some of his deposits. Then I remembered the lovely quilt I saw that day in your kitchen, and all the pieces fit together."

Payne reached into his pocket again. An icy, cold fear enveloped Jamie.

"This, by the way, was worthless." Payne held up Jamie's drawing of the quilt, then released it. The paper fluttered to the floor.

Suddenly the phone rang. Payne swung around, then back quickly. After a while, it fell silent.

Jamie and Kevin exchanged glances. Maybe it was Mom or better yet, Officer Stephens. When they didn't answer, he'd come see what was the matter. If they could only keep Payne there.

"Get the coins," Payne snapped.

Jamie gathered them slowly. For a moment she considered throwing them at him.

"I'm really in a bit of a hurry. I have an appointment to sell a house," Payne said, then chuckled. "Your mother has been incredibly helpful."

He held up a key. "This will give me a chance to get well away without any further interference from you brats."

"You're going to lock us in the attic?" Jamie asked, eyeing the strange key.

"Not necessarily. This is a skeleton key — it fits the tower, too."

Payne motioned for them to go up the steps to the tower.

Jamie and Kevin backed away from him as slowly as they could manage.

When they got up the steps, Payne slammed the door shut.

They heard the key turn, then footsteps rapidly fading as Payne hurried away.

14

Jamie listened to the car start and drive away. She finally let the tears roll down her cheeks.

"Where did that key come from?" Kevin asked.

Jamie shook her head. "I've never seen it before. It must be a passkey — that's probably how he's robbed all those houses of their antiques."

Jamie tried to wipe the tears from her face.

Kevin walked over and jiggled the doorknob a few times. It was locked tight.

Jamie finally looked down at the leather-bound book she had taken from Payne before he had moved them to the tower. She flipped through it. But Payne was right. Nothing in there could help them now.

"Kevin, we've got to do something! We've got to get out of here! Mom is going to sign that contract and Payne is going to get away. . . ."

"What do you suggest?"

"I don't know." Jamie walked around and around the tower.

"I'll try to break the door down," Kevin said.

"This is an old sturdy house. You can't break the door down."

"You're probably right. Besides, I don't have any room to get a run at it," Kevin said.

"You watch too much television," said Jamie.

Kevin sat down in the middle of the floor. He reached up and grabbed Jamie's hand.

"Let's just enjoy being locked up this time. Someone, Dan or your Mom, will show up soon. And I can't think of anyone I'd rather be locked up with," Kevin said softly.

Jamie stared hard at Kevin. "How can you even suggest such a thing? That man is trying to take my house."

"Jamie, you have a one-track mind. All you ever talk about is this house. What about my mom? A scandal like Payne threatened would ruin her. What about *your* mom? She's tired of taking care of this place. And what about me? I'm trying to tell you how much I like you and you won't even listen. It's not easy to get up the nerve to tell a girl a thing like that."

Jamie dropped down beside Kevin. Tears rolled down her cheeks again.

"I thought you understood," she said, sobbing.

"Jamie, I do," Kevin assured her.

"Then why are you just giving up? Why aren't you helping me get out of here, so I can get to Mom before Payne does?"

"Payne means what he says, Jamie. He will do all those things he said he would."

"I think Mom and Officer Stephens will believe us," Jamie said, her tears drying up now. "I'm sure they will — and we have the ledger!"

Jamie held it up. "He shouldn't have left it. It proves there was money here, that we didn't make it up."

Jamie jumped to her feet.

Kevin rose more slowly, but she could tell he was thinking about what she'd said.

"Who'd believe that your mom would sell stolen goods? I don't believe it!" Jamie kept on, trying to convince Kevin.

"You're right!" he finally said. "Let's get out of here!"

Kevin looked out the window. "I don't think I could get all the way down even if we broke the window," he said.

"Is there anyone out there? We could yell and try to get their attention," Jamie suggested.

"It's pretty dark. There aren't many people even driving by, much less walking."

"It is dark," Jamie said looking out. "Where's Mom? Where's Dan?"

Jamie went over to the door and examined the lock carefully.

"A skeleton key? He said it was a skeleton key, right?" Jamie said, excitement edging her voice.

"That's what he said."

"Kevin, we can pick the lock. Officer Stephens said it was easy to pick old locks like that."

"Did he tell you how?"

"No, but what harm is there in trying? Let's see, we need something that will fit in the hole."

"A bobby pin? That's what they use in books," Kevin said.

Jamie pulled up the lids on the window seats, searching for something, anything.

"A little screwdriver!" Jamie held it up. "Mom never puts anything away, thank heavens."

Jamie inserted it in the keyhole and rattled it around.

"Let me try," Kevin said, pushing her gently out of the way.

She watched quietly as her friend moved the screwdriver in every direction.

When she couldn't stand waiting and doing nothing one more second, Jamie asked Kevin for another chance to try.

Kevin took the screwdriver out of the lock and slapped it into Jamie's outstretched hand. He moved back and crossed his arms.

Jamie took the screws out of the doorknob, pulled

the knob out, reached her fingers down, and turned the locking mechanism.

Kevin's arms dropped to his sides. His eyes lit up and a smile spread across his face. "Nothing like using a tool for what it was meant to be used for," he said. "But I sure am glad you didn't have to draw our way out."

He held up Jamie's quilt picture. The corners of his lips twitched with the effort not to smile.

Jamie grabbed the picture and stuffed it into the ledger.

Kevin ran down the short flight of stairs leading into the library.

Jamie followed right behind him.

At the door to the library, Kevin halted abruptly, causing Jamie to collide with him.

Jamie opened her mouth to ask what he was doing, but Kevin clamped his hand over it before she could say anything. He tilted his head toward the stairs leading to the main floor of the house.

Jamie listened carefully, but heard nothing. She tried to pull away.

Kevin shook his head and motioned downstairs again.

Jamie strained her ears. This time she heard someone, and from the heavy sound of the steps she guessed it was a man, moving from room to room.

A tiny knot of fear pulled itself tight inside Jamie's stomach: Perhaps Mr. Payne hadn't left at all. Anyone who had any legitimate business there would have given them some sign.

She pointed back to the tower.

Tiptoeing, they climbed the steps. Jamie headed to the window seat, raised the lid, and threw one leg over the edge, tucking herself inside. Before lowering the lid, she indicated that Kevin should do the same.

In the darkness, once again, Jamie waited.

15

Jamie listened as someone climbed the stairs, then walked down the upstairs hallway. Footsteps faded, then got louder. She heard him come into the library, then climb the steps to the tower.

The footsteps came toward her then stopped.

"Where can those kids be?" Jamie heard a familiar voice say as though he was thoroughly put out.

She slowly pushed up the lid of the window seat.

Officer Stephens crouched, then whirled about.

Anger gathered in his eyes. "Where have you been? Playing games? You called me, then called your mom and said it was an emergency. We couldn't find you anywhere!"

Officer Stephens leaned forward and grabbed Jamie's arm, pulling her none too gently out of the window seat.

Kevin chose that moment to pop-up out of his hiding place.

"This is not funny!" the policeman said, giving

the two of them equally dark looks.

"It's no game," Jamie hastily assured him. "Mr. Payne locked us up in the tower and, when we got out and heard someone downstairs, we were scared he might still be in the house. So we came back up here and hid."

"Payne locked you up here! C'mon, Jamie, you expect me to believe that?"

"I most certainly do. Come with me," Jamie ordered confidently. "Why would we take apart the lock to get out if we weren't locked in?" she pointed out as they passed by the door.

Jamie marched down the stairs, out of the library, down the hall, and up the stairs to the attic.

"Look!" She pointed at the practically empty room.

"There's nothing here," said Officer Stephens.

"That's just it. Payne took everything. He has it in a truck in a garage behind his office. We were there."

The policeman looked at Jamie, then at Kevin.

"You're serious," he said.

"It's true," Kevin put in.

Officer Stephens turned and quickly made his way down the stairs to the phone.

Jamie and Kevin followed.

Officer Stephens was hanging up the phone by the time they joined him.

"Stay right here," he said sternly. "I'll let you

know as soon as something happens."

Jamie looked at the floor. She wasn't about to make any promises.

Stephens rushed out, slamming the door.

"What now?" Kevin asked.

Jamie watched out the window until the police car was out of sight. Without a word she picked up Kevin's coat and tossed it to him, then slipped into her own.

"Jamie, Payne had a head start. I don't want you to be too disappointed if he's already gotten rid of the stuff in the garage."

Jamie smiled. "He won't get far."

She opened the door and waved Kevin out.

"Huh?"

"I let the air out of one of the tires on the truck."

16

By the time they arrived at the garage, a small crowd had gathered. Police cars, with their lights flashing, lined the street leading to the alley.

Jamie and Kevin pushed and squirmed their way through to the front of the crowd.

A feeling of satisfaction raged through Jamie when she caught a glimpse of Payne sitting in the back seat of a police car.

It was only a short time before Officer Stephens noticed them.

"I should've locked you both up again when I left," he said, coming over to join them.

"Good job, Officer Stephens," Jamie said. She held out her hand to congratulate him.

"You can call me Dan from now on," he said, shaking Jamie's hand. "Besides, I couldn't have done it without a little help," Dan added, winking at her, then jerking his thumb toward the truck. "Old Mr. Payne tried to drive off, but after he hit a couple of those ruts his flat tire split and peeled right off. But I don't suppose you had anything to do with that flat tire, right?"

Jamie had seldom felt as proud of herself as she did when she saw the panel truck slouched over to one side.

Kevin put his arm around her and squeezed her shoulder.

"Did you get the coins?" Jamie asked.

"What coins?"

Jamie groaned. "We forgot to tell you. We found some gold coins in the tower and Mr. Payne took them. They were in a brown bank bag. It was pretty heavy, but not real full."

"They weren't on Payne," Dan said.

"Can we look in the garage? Please?" she pleaded.

He faced the garage, crawling with police. Turning slowly, he nodded. "Let me clear it, but since you did have a hand in catching the guy, I don't see why not. You may have to wait a while though."

Jamie danced with impatience as she watched Officer Stephens talk to a man wearing a wrinkled, plaid suit. He finally beckoned to them to come over.

"This is Detective Owens," Dan said.

The detective looked them over from head to toe. "So you're the kid that let the air out of the tire?"

144

Before Jamie could form an answer, Owens continued, "Good thing you did. He had the truck loaded and would have been out of here otherwise."

Jamie looked the man in the face. He had blue eyes that were twinkling merrily. He smiled at her and patted her on the head.

"Go on in and look around, but don't touch anything without clearing it with Stephens. We're working on the truck now, so stay out of the way."

Jamie and Kevin went inside the garage, leaving Dan lounging in the doorway.

Furniture was scattered everywhere. Chairs lay on their sides. Table legs stuck up in the air. Desk drawers hung open.

For the second time that day, they circled the garage.

It was hard to see anything much, Jamie thought, given the conditions. By the time they had gone around three times, Jamie was ready to give up. She started toward Dan.

But as Jamie passed by the open doors of the panel truck, something familiar caught her eye. She backtracked to get a better look.

"Kevin! Dan!" Jamie called, a sense of urgency in her voice.

They hurried to her side.

"Isn't that the other desk — the one that was like my tower desk but with square legs?" She pointed at a desk nestled among an array of furniture. "Remember, Kevin? We had to figure out which one was the one that matched the quilt."

"It sure looks like it," Kevin agreed.

"Do you think I could examine it up close?" Jamie asked Dan.

"Sure."

Luckily, Jamie thought, the drawers faced the open end of the truck.

She climbed up, wedging her body between the desk and a sofa.

Jamie pulled out the large middle drawer and gently pushed on the bottom of it. She swallowed her disappointment when the bottom appeared solid.

She tried the top side drawer with the same result.

The third drawer she tried didn't open at first. Jamie pulled again. The drawer slid out, then stuck. She worked patiently, rocking it from side to side until she could get her hand in it.

At first touch, the bottom felt as snug as all the others. Jamie ran her finger tips over it again and was rewarded with just a tiny depression. She pushed down and back and the bottom gave way. The bank bag rested underneath.

17

Kevin thrust a big, wrapped box with a bow on top at Jamie as soon as she answered the door. Then he gave a low whistle of approval as soon as he stepped inside and got a good look at her.

Jamie curtsied slightly and turned around, modeling her red sweater and plaid skirt. Maybe it wasn't Cindy and Mom's blue satin, but it was right for her.

"Just look what I have to compete with!" Jamie laughed as Cindy flitted into the hall in her fairy costume and did a graceful pirouette.

"What's in the package?" Cindy asked as soon as she finished her turn.

"It's for Jamie. From me and Dan, sort of." He guided Jamie into the living room, where her mother and Dan were waiting.

Jamie looked at it for a few moments, then tore into the wrapping paper. When she saw what was inside, she became absolutely still.

"My quilt!" she murmured.

Very gently, she shook it out and spread it across the sofa.

"And that's not all, honey," Mom said. "We're going to get the coins back, very soon."

Kevin and Dan hung back, saying nothing, to give Jamie time to absorb the information.

Jamie looked at her friends. She felt like she might burst, she was so happy. "How can I thank you?" she said.

"You've already thanked me," Kevin said. "Getting me through math. What a relief!"

Jamie leaned over and hugged Kevin. She felt very proud of herself because she didn't blush when she did it.

"Tell me again, slowly, where the money came from," Dan said. "I still don't think I have it straight."

Mom, Kevin, and Cindy groaned, while a great smile crossed Jamie's face. They had heard the story about a million times by now.

Mom pulled Cindy onto her lap. "We'd better sit down," she said.

"It really took the letters, the quilt, and the ledger to piece the whole thing together," Jamie began.

"In the letters, Great-Grandpa George dropped clues to his wife that he was hiding the money, but you wouldn't know that unless you knew there was money to hide and that was in the ledger, which he had hidden someplace else. The ledger also served as a sort of diary. The clues to where the money was hidden were on the quilt — the rainbow and the gold."

"Where did he get the money and why didn't he just put it in the bank?" Dan asked.

"Some of the money came from the feed store. He was still running that just like he always did. He was saving every extra cent and eating very little, not using any heat, walking everywhere. We read that in his letters. But George had a second job, one that he wasn't so proud of. It took him all over the place doing odd things at odd hours. The reason Great-Grandfather didn't tell anyone about his other job was because he was working for the funeral home — picking up bodies, digging graves, making coffins."

"Gross!" Cindy said.

"He didn't want to put his money in the bank because it had failed once and he'd just about lost everything. He also kept all his money in gold — cold hard cash. Whenever he got greenbacks, he immediately exchanged them for gold. That was fine until they passed a law making it illegal for citizens to own or trade in gold. But that still didn't stop George. He kept exchanging his currency for gold, only on the black market.

"That made him even *more* secretive, because

he felt uneasy about some of those transactions and some of the people he was dealing with. He started to hide the gold in the window seat."

Jamie paused for breath.

"Why didn't he ever use the money?" Dan asked.

"He died. He got pneumonia and died. Elizabeth came home and took over the feed store. She kept the letters, but I guess she never found George's ledger. He had recorded all the money he made, how he made it, and where he spent it. And whenever George added gold to his window seat bank, he drew a little rainbow next to the deposit written in the ledger," Jamie answered.

"I guess this just goes to show you can believe some of those stories about old houses. It almost paid off for Mr. Payne," Dan said.

"When do you think we will get the coins?" Jamie asked.

"I'm not sure, but it won't be too long," Dan said.

"Mom," Jamie began thoughtfully.

Dan, Kevin, Cindy, and Mom exchanged looks.

"Now that we know from Great-Grandfather's ledger that he didn't do anything wrong to get the money — except keep the gold when he should have turned it in — I was thinking. The coins are worth more than just their face value, you know. I looked them up in a coin catalog. We can get a pretty good amount for them. . . ."

She paused a moment, then plunged back in. "Why don't we use the money to fix the house, now that we're going to keep it? That woman called again from the Historical Society and asked us if we were planning to be on their tour. I want to have the house ready by then."

Dan cleared his throat. "Kevin and I've been talking about that. Maybe we could help you out a little with some of the work."

Jamie threw her arms around him and gave him a huge hug.

Mom sighed. "Jamie, I'm leaving this house renovation up to you. You're the one who believed in the story and I can't imagine your great-grandfather wanting to see the money spent on anything more than this house. We'll do whatever you want to do with the coins.

"Within reason, of course," Mom added. "And now we are going to eat or we'll be late for Cindy's play."

Everyone trooped into the dining room except Jamie. She could scarcely tear herself away from the quilt and her visions of the house and how it was going to look when she was finished fixing it up.

Cindy returned and tugged on Jamie's hand. "C'mon, the food is getting cold."

Jamie leaned over and straightened Cindy's crown, then let her lead her to the table.

About the Author

VICKI BERGER ERWIN, a graduate of the University of Missouri, lives in Kirkwood, Missouri, with her husband Jim and their two children. She loves quilts and she attends every quilt show within driving distance. This is her first novel.

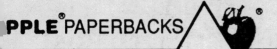

Collect Them All!

by Ann M. Martin

The seven girls at Stoneybrook Middle School get into all kinds of adventures...with school, boys, and, of course, baby-sitting!